S 190M 6/78 CTW&SL

AMAZING GRACE

AMAZING GRACE

Alida Baxter

Arlington Books
Clifford Street Mayfair
London

AMAZING GRACE
first published 1979 by
Arlington Books (Publishers) Ltd
3 Clifford Street Mayfair
London W1

Typeset by Inforum Ltd Portsmouth
Printed and bound in England by
Billing & Sons Limited
Guildford, Worcester and London

British Library Cataloguing in Publication Data
Baxter, Alida
Amazing Grace
I. Title
823'.9'.1F PR6052.A847A/
ISBN 0-85140-326-3

This book is for Desmond Elliott

Who always does at least six
impossible things before breakfast –
some of them to other publishers.

Part One

The Hopeful Society of Faith in the Continual Resurrection: an unspoiled and Godly settlement, lying mid-way between Paradise and Intercourse, and within buggy reach of Bird in Hand, in the County of Lancaster, Pennsylvania.

I

Sister Lorelei broke through her arthritis, and brought down her fist to smash its reflection in the pale honey mirror of the polished table top.

"Thee knows we're right, Mother! *Show the World thy back and keep thy front for the Hopeful* – there it stands, plain as anything in the Book!"

"The Phrasebook of Uplift was composed long ago, under *entirely* different –"

"Thee aren't saying we should throw away the sacred writings of Elder Albert?"

There was a shivering all round the table – a twitching, and a fingering at the napes of the craning necks, where occasional wisps of hair escaped beneath the blue linen caps. Most of the stray hair was grey. And the eyes that watched and blinked were encircled with sundials of lines. Some backs were straighter than others, some fronts more curvaceous. Bosoms heaved excitedly against the blue linen bodices and strained at the white pinafores – like the muzzles of creatures scenting water, Mother Germaine thought irritably. Oh, *women* – why were they so difficult? And why in the name of goodness did poor Brother Orville have to die.

"Sisters, Eldresses, let us be calm. Of course I am not saying that we should throw away the writings. All I am saying, is they're too narrow for this case. Elder Albert composed the Phrasebook more than a hundred years ago. He set down tenets to guide us –"

"Thee admits it!" announced Lorelei.

Sister Agatha clutched at her blue linen cap. "Thou admittest!" she shrieked. "Thou admittest! *Thou admittest*! If I have to sit here one more minute and listen to that reformed houri massacring the language –"

"Sisters! Sisters!"

"Reformed houri." Lorelei retreated behind her wrinkled dignity. "Whatever that is, I bet thee's trying to say something bad to me. Just because *I* don't sit reading dictionaries all the Recreation Hour."

"I do not sit reading only dictionaries!"

"No, thee reads all the murders out of the Intercourse Review! It's too much for my insides, Agatha. I have to go and lie down. The way thee goes on about the blood, I could bring up my Shoo Fly Pie."

"Anybody could bring up thy Shoo Fly Pie. It has nothing to do with death, Lorelei, it has to do with too much molasses."

"*Sisters*!" Mother Germaine could feel distinctly that her face was going red. "Please let us return to the matter we were discussing!"

Sister Agatha pursed her lips. Sister Amy gazed out of the window. Someone (Lorelei?) sniffed. A chair or two grated on the shining wood-block flooring.

"As I was saying –" A careful pause, to see that she had their attention. "As I was saying, when Elder Albert composed the Uplifting Phrases our whole situation was quite different. The Society had so many converts – many more than were ever accepted – and there were all the foundlings. The numbers of foundlings the settlement took in! Who was to know that in a hundred years there wouldn't be any more foundlings? How could Elder Albert have set down a Phrase for our guidance? How could he have foreseen the way things would change? How could he have foreseen –" she swallowed hard and closed her eyes. "*Contraception.*"

"Oh, well, said Sister Amy.

Sister Heloise began to cry.

"He lay there on his death bed, composing the Phrasebook –"

"He should have foreseen contraception." Sister Agatha looked troubled. "He lay there long enough."

Mother Germaine shot her a glare. "*As I was saying*, he lay on his death bed –"

"For the whole of eighteen seventy-six."

"Yes, Agatha, indeed, and that was *a very long time ago.* No contraception, dearest Sister. And no socially acceptable one parent families!"

"Thou dost not say! Hark at that," huffed Agatha. "Didst thou buy a copy of the *New York Times* again?"

I will not strike her, seethed Mother Germaine. I will remember the blessed teachings – *A Hopeful countenance is a cheerful contenance, even at a burial. Hopefuls recall Lazarus.* She took a deep breath. "Yes, dearest Sister, I have had occasion during the past months of Brother Orville's illness to give deep consideration to our future, should he pass away. Now that he has –"

Sister Heloise let out a sob.

"– leaving no issue –"

Sister Heloise threw her apron over her head and rushed from the room.

"I honestly cannot see that we have any alternative."

"No alternative!" Silent till now, Sister Unity erupted like an avenging Valkyrie. "No alternative to sending two unsullied innocents out into the World to meet the Lord alone knows what? How *couldst* thou, Mother? Dost thou not remember our meeting only ten days ago? In this very room –" She flung back her arm and struck a white blind so that it shot up the window. "After Titty came back from Paradise with –"

"Oh, really, oh I can't stand it!" moaned Lorelei.

"Those *things* – what did the carton say?"

Sister Agatha studied the ceiling. "Internal sanitary protection."

"Internal sanitary protection! A hideous device to ensnare pure womanhood. A work of the unclean. An engine of the Devil! Didst thou ever see anything like it in all thy life!"

"Yes," said Sister Agatha. "But I've also read Havelock Ellis." She became, for the moment, the centre of attention.

Sister Lorelei said resentfully, "I don't know what that means, I'm sure. Thee's just trying to be too clever again."

"*Sisters*!"

Sister Amy crossed her legs and said, "You can't get Havelock

Ellis at a drug store."

"Precisely!" Unity snapped. "Titty went with Heloise to sell quilts. Heloise let her go into the store for an ice-cream. Five minutes, Mother! And what did she come back with?"

Lorelei fanned herself arthritically with her apron.

"An engine of Satan! I must protest, and I warn thee, Mother –"

Mother Germaine groaned.

"The Devil lurks in wait out there at every soda fountain!" Unity threw herself back into her chair with a death-rattle of stiffened pinafore.

Of course, it's Mercy doing the laundry this week, Mother Germaine remembered wildly. That girl's always so generous with the starch.

There was a deceptive lull; beneath the silence came a layer of heavy breathing, the rustle of clothes and an indignant snort or cough. The faces – some reflected in the table – were such good faces, their superior told herself firmly, but at present some looked adamant and some looked cross. Sister Amy was adamant in her passivity, her broad, smooth, rosy countenance philosophic. Sister Lorelei sat twitching crossly at her apron, her wrinkled mouth forming a sulky cupid's bow. Sister Agatha crouched in her chair, a wise and wizened old squirrel, and Sister Unity vibrated energy remorseless as radium – pulsating, unrelenting, across the room – her pale eyes wide and accusing, her perfect nose white, her fearless brow cleaving waves no-one could see.

And what of poor shy Heloise? Mother Germaine wondered. Is she up in her room writing more of those letters to her pen friend?

Useless and idle, this sort of thinking. She smoothed her sleeves and pulled her cuffs straight. "The Devil may lurk in wait, Sister Unity, but one is not necessarily obliged to keep the appointment."

Chins rose to the right of her, chins rose to the left of her. Sister Amy glanced towards Heaven and a framed sampler, which hung in cross-stiched exhortation between the windows. *Never refuse money*, it read. *It can always be washed*.

"Dear Sisters –" Mother Germaine forced her face into a patient expression. "I fear we must be realistic. Our last dear Brother, poor dear Orville, has died. A loss. A really dreadful loss. None of us actually asked him to fix those shingles, but then, there it is, he always did have that selfless nature, though what with the mumps and the collitis he should never have gone up on that roof. A tragedy, a really tragic loss, not only of a good man, but Sisters, he was the last man we had!"

She looked round them all, earnestly, to see whether this had sunk in. "The Hopeful Society, Sisters, is facing a fatal crisis. We haven't had a convert – of either sex – for years! Not since Sister Unity, and that was *decades* ago."

Unity eviscerated her with a steel stare; she had been maintaining she was forty-three for at least the last twenty years now. Mother Germaine flinched slightly, tugged at her cap and soldiered on. "As I was saying, we've had no converts, and as to foundlings – we haven't been blessed with a foundling since we found Chastity." Her cap dipped. "And we only got Titty because her mother was drunk – yes, and wandered away from the road! Sisters, if we go on as we are the Faith will die with us. We are a lonely band of women – and how many years do we have left? Surely the answer is to go out into the World and seek converts – male converts, they must be male converts. Surely the answer is to send out missionaries."

Sister Agatha pursed her lips and also, somewhat alarmingly, she pursed her nose. "Elder Albert never wrote a word that I've read about sending out missionaries."

"Elder Albert," fumed Mother Germaine, "did not *found* this Society, *Sister dear*."

Agatha shrugged, and her bones tinkled.

"When Elder Albert took to his death bed this Society had already been in existence for one hundred years. If he hadn't taken so long to die he might never have written the Phrases, but there'd still have been a Hopeful Society." The superior breast swelled with pride. "Elder Albert was indeed inspired with the Blessed Word for his composition, but the Society was founded by two women – remember that, Sisters, two English *women* – who travelled far, braving untold dangers, the storms of the Atlantic –" She waved descriptively. "Moral and physical peril, disease, penury, opprobrium, and who settled here –"

Sister Amy sniffed. "Because the wheel came off the wagon."

"Whatever the cause, Sister Amy, they chose to settle here! Are we more timid than they were, two hundred years farther on? And with plumbing inside the house? Come now, Sisters. When the Society's future is at stake, are we to put thought of self before thought of the Society? Are we to say that such a task is too great for us? Remember the Phrasebook of Uplift: *No field is too large for the Hopeful plough*."

"The Phrasebook also says," that was Unity, very coldly, "*If thou shakest hands with the World, count thou thy fingers afterwards*."

"But we already shake! I mean, we already deal with the World, Sister Unity. Don't we go into Paradise, and Intercourse, to trade?"

"Yes, Mother, and when we do, see what happens! Children like Titty are exposed to the contamination of infernal machines!"

"Children like Titty are, of course, impressionable. I had never intended sending out Titty." She folded her hands in prayer beneath the table. "I had thought of sending out our two previous foundlings –" A gulp. "I had intended sending out Grace and Mercy."

There was a measureless, paralysed, motionless silence. Followed by a harmonised chorus of agonised shrieks.

Sister Lorelei grappled out a small phial and inhaled, gasping, till the tears ran along her wrinkles and found their way down her channelled face.

Even Amy raised an eyebrow. "Grace and Mercy aren't ever –" she said, and was vanquished by Unity.

Unity had leapt up again. "Grace and Mercy mustn't ever go out to trade! We decided that at a Recreation Hour – dost thou not remember, Mother? Five years ago, six years this September, when we saw how they were developing. We cannot, we must not –"

Mother Germaine held her knees together and prayed fervently for moral strength. Sister Unity, infuriatingly, and as usual, was perfectly right.

When Grace's shape had become impossible to hide, and even

had an astonishing effect under coarse, starched, serviceable linen, when her glossy auburn hair crept out of her cap and curled down her neck in uncontrollable ringlets; when Mercy's long, silky, dark blonde eyelashes cast semi-circular shadows on her perfect, peachy cheeks, and her lips darkened and her hips rounded, and she began begging for combs to hold up the weight of her waist-length blonde braids; when both girls had straight, white teeth and curved, moist mouths, and dimples . . . Then it was decided that the only way to keep them safe from the World was to keep them at home.

How many trips to Paradise and Intercourse before they got rid of more than their quilts?

It was not a sufficient precaution, cutting off their hair. And, besides, their hair had grown again, very rapidly.

Of all the Sisterhood, they were the only ones who were never allowed farther than the simple white fencing that bordered the settlement land. To the east they were restricted to a sight of the track that led through the green, undulating fields to the Paradise road. To the west they could see the rolling woods, but they were never permitted to walk there alone.

And it was these two, who for so long had been so specially protected, and whose only recollection of teeming commerce could be the Kitchen Kettle shops in Intercourse – it was these two who should now be sent forth, to meet unnameable trials and temptations, to deal with the World on its own ground, to set foot where no Sister's laced boot had ever trod.

Mother Germaine trembled within at her own temerity. "I have given," she quavered through the uproar, "this matter very careful thought. And I do feel," her tone strengthened, "that Grace and Mercy are more likely to bring back a vir – er, a *young* – er, a *male* convert, than any of the rest of us."

The Eldresses stared at her, quiet now for a moment, and she felt herself flush, knowing too well what they could see. Her long face, that might once have been handsome. Her strong, straight nose and large, dark brown eyes. All collapsing daily, lower and lower, over the edge of her jaw and into her neck.

It still shocked her, this business of ageing – that whenever she caught a glimpse of herself in a window pane or a polished surface the reflection was so unexpectedly *old*. The pouched, loose-lidded eyes and blurred chin of an old woman. The grey eyebrows and the slack cheeks.

She brought her hands out from under the table, and clasped them in front of her. Dark oval age spots and knobbly gaunt knuckles. She blinked, and lifted her gaze to the watching Sisterhood. United in their disapproval, wary, embattled, uncertain: Lorelei, arthritic and sniffing; Agatha, brown and seamed as walnut; Unity, a Nordic old maiden; Amy, red-veined, placid and plain. Would Heloise, too, have been on their side, with them? Weepy, flat-chested, wan, worn, antique Heloise?

"Well?" She cleared her throat and squared her tired shoulders. And the Sisters moved awkwardly, as if in response, in their seats. "Well?" she said. "Eldresses?"

They looked from one to another, starting to speak and then falling silent. And then they looked back at her. And then they looked at their laps.

"More likely to bring back a man, um?" murmured Amy.

Lorelei dried her eyes and restoppered her phial, and shot a sideways sneer at gnarled Agatha. "Lord help us all, Mother," she sniffed. "But thee's probably right."

II

The two girls sat on the bench outside the summer kitchen. It was not summer (it was not even full spring yet) but they used the cool, stone-flagged summer kitchen when they were doing the Hopeful's laundry. It was a chore for which they needed all the cool they could get.

They had pummelled clothes and linen in, and hauled wet clothes and linen out, of the bottled-gas-driven Maytag washing machine; they had scrubbed and boiled and rinsed and starched and wrung; they had struggled with baskets, and pegged out sheets and towels and pillow-slips and long cotton drawers; they had heated the heavy flat irons and brought in what was ironable, and ironed. And now they sat on the low bench and wilted, while the blue dresses flapped on the line under the maples and the irons were heating again on the dark old chimneyed stove.

The redhead had pulled off her cap and dangled it limply by its strings from her fingers. "I'm going to die. I am going to *die*," she said.

"Ooo, no, thee aren't! Please don't say such things, Grace, it's wicked. Being tired doesn't feel good," the blonde clutched the bench, "but it's not being *dead*."

Grace pouted a minute. Then she said, "All right, thou be tired. I'll be dead."

"Ooo, stop that! Thee knows it's sinful, thee knows we're forbidden to say those things." And Mercy glanced round frantically as though someone might have crept up upon them, and heard.

"Yes, well, I suppose I shouldn't." The unrepentant redhead began unlacing her bodice and blowing down it, spreading the pale beads of sweat. "What with poor old Brother Orville hardly cold in his grave."

Mercy's huge blue eyes instantly filled and brimmed over with tears. The corners of her sweet pink mouth crumpled and a line of moisture ran out of her nose. Her little hands stopped beating the air and grabbed at one-another. "Oh, *poor* Brother Orville!" she wailed. "He never harmed anyone!"

Grace found a knot in her laces and cursed (not out loud – not in front of Mercy). Out loud she said grumpily, "I'm sorry I mentioned it." And "He's better off where he is."

"But that poor old man –"

"Mercy, that is not the Hopeful way. Remember what it says in the Phrases of Uplift, think of Lazarus. Oh, what the –" And she burst her laces. Fortunately, Mercy didn't notice; she was ransacking her apron for a clean handkerchief. And sobbing.

"Nobody raised poor old Brother Orville!"

"That's just what I heard," said Grace. With a wriggle, she made herself more comfortable on the bench, and hoiked her skirts up over her knees; she wiped at her forehead, lifted the mass of hair that had come down loose on her shoulders and fashioned an auburn pillow of it behind her head; leant back against the white painted clapboard wall of the house, and stretched out her legs till she'd made gravel foot rests with the heels of her boots. The cool air swirled around her neck and into her undone bodice; it rushed up under her lifted skirts and she sighed thankfully.

Beside her, the blonde mourner moped. "Does th-thee really th-think th-thee should sit like that?" she snivelled.

"No. But I'm doing it anyway."

"It l-looks so *flagrant*, Grace. It l-looks so *Worldly*."

Grace shrugged her pearly slopes and rises.

"C-couldn't th-thee p-put down thy skirts? Grace, it doesn't l-look *chaste*."

"Oh, well." Grace pulled a face at the maples. "I don't care what it looks like, because I know we're chaste." Defiantly, she spread her legs wider. "If there's anything we are, Mercy, it's chaste. I bet there haven't been any two girls in the whole history of the world who've been as chaste as we are. There wouldn't have been any history if everyone in the world had been this chaste."

"Ooo, Grace –"

"I'm so chaste I can't stand it. I'm so chaste I think I'm going to *die*." And she crunched her boot-heels in the heaped gravel, and bulged alarmingly through her open bodice.

* * *

Given that the girls side by side on the bench (one cowering and one furious) were roughly the same age (both about eighteen, as near as was known), had been found within a few months of each other and brought up by the same Sisters, in the same small community, the disparity in their characters was enough to give a geneticist wet dreams.

Grace had a moonlit skin and a twenty-four hour libido, while Mercy blushed every time she heard a cock crowing, and took baths wearing a petticoat.

At the age of five, Grace had been found staring at the Intercourse store-side graffiti, and was later discovered not only to have understood but also to have memorised every word.

Mercy fainted when Sister Agatha explained to her gently what the term "with child" meant.

At the age of ten, Grace was seen riding the milk cow, and when taxed by Mother Germaine said boldly that she liked the feeling.

Mercy would not even climb up in the buggy because it meant lifting her skirts.

From the time she could walk, Grace would be traced to wherever in the settlement animals might be mating; there she would stand, chubby hands applauding in ecstasy, little face entranced.

Mercy, when she was told where they came from, refused to eat eggs and then threw up her milk.

Whilst Mercy was not merely content with her restricted situation but actually moved about with her eyes down, in case they should light upon the unHopeful great outdoors, Grace was very discontent indeed, and showed it.

At thirteen, when her requests to go and sell quilts were refused obdurately, she had shaken a drum of pepper into the beef stew and two bottles of laxative had gone in the Shoo Fly Pie.

Confined within the white fencing – denied Paradise *and* Intercourse – over the years she had let the Society know exactly how she felt. Enjoying a rebellious puberty, she cut all the fur off Mother Germaine's cat. She painted an obscene word on the cow, chased the chickens till they were egg-bound, cut down the clothes lines, climbed on the roof stark naked and burned huge holes in the entire Sisterhood's drawers.

And she tried to run away, but every time she tried Mercy snitched.

Then, abruptly, when she was fifteen she gave up all these industries. Instead she settled for a sultry, silent smouldering, and relieving bursts of dancing in the Recreation Hour. For the time being her inventive fury was exhausted. And besides, she had a crush on Unity.

So she went about her work, and did it correctly and neatly, and learned all of the Phrases that she hadn't yet learned off by heart. And when Sister Agatha played the piano in the evening she got up and danced like a wanton, and cast glances over her shoulder at pale, blazing Unity.

The beloved, for her part, was quite oblivious. She did not notice the collars that were starched and pressed into glistening halos, nor the extra polish lavished in the Eldresses' Room that she shared. She was blind to the steps that were scrubbed and the grates that were cleaned to her glory, and she regarded Grace as the others did – as a necessarily protected child.

Meanwhile, the child throbbed about the place, craving to be unprotected, and slaving off an incredible amount of sexual energy.

And every time it looked as though Grace's Grand Passion were dying, some twist of Fate would wring a kind word, or touch, or a special favour from Unity. And thus niggardly reimbursed the Grand Passion would flare up again.

It was only during the past winter that Grace had finally ceased repining.

She had helped to nurse her idol through the grippe, and Unity had looked very ugly. Seeing the beloved red-nosed and sweaty (not to mention washing out the sputum cups and carrying the bed pans and boiling the pale green handkerchiefs) had dealt Grace's feelings a body-blow.

As a result she became unsettled, and had since by turns been either too quiet or too restless – either unable to keep still or keeping still for hours, hunched over a book.

The books contained, in a few cases, sepia pictures, of the Milky Way and unclothed savages, and lately Grace had more than once wondered to Mercy just how far away the savages might be.

"I'm so chaste," she said again now, "I can't stand it! I'm so chaste I think I'm going to *die*!"

And crunching across the gravel came Heloise.

III

"Thee's been smoking." A high-pitched accusing whisper came from quaking Mercy. "Thee's been rolling those cigarlettes."

"Cigarettes. And no I haven't, not in ages."

They were standing, waiting, in the hall outside the Eldresses' Meeting Room. Sister Heloise had fetched them, but they did not yet know for what purpose. And Mercy, with some drama, had convinced herself they were to be chastised.

"Ooooo!" she squeaked.

"Now what?"

"Thy bodice – Grace, all thy bosom's exposed!"

"Not all of it, only about three-quarters." In an effort to fasten up her front again, Grace had been wrenching at the torn ends of her laces. Now she tugged even harder. For a moment the linen edges came together. "Well, thank –"

There was a truly dreadful tearing sound.

"Oooooo!"

"Oh well."

"We can't go and see Mother Germaine with thy bodice open!"

"Why not? Is my bosom going to leap out and prevent thee?"

"Grace, Grace, thee'll go to Hell! Thee'll suffer eternal damnation!"

"Just because I've got a bosom?"

"Oooooo, hasn't thee any shame!"

The latch rattled, and stopped the redhead replying. As the door swung open she held her breath and took a grip on her bodice – her attitude, when Mother Germaine saw her, was startlingly like that of a soldier propped up on a tomb.

"Er –" said the Mother. "Girls!" And ushered them busily in.

The room, except for table and chairs, was virtually empty (the Hopefuls do not believe in cluttered houses) but the quality of the polished wood gave it warmth and character, and Mother Germaine's wide, rather nervous smiles and be-seated gestures swam, repeated, in the honey mirror furniture.

"Sit down!" she said. "Sit down, dears. My, my, but it's a long time since we had a good talk."

Grace and Mercy exchanged apprehensive glances. The last good talk had been about politeness to Eldresses, as in not eating the last slice of ham before an arthritic hand could get a fork in it.

"Yes," said Mother Germaine, beaming rigidly at her victims. "It really has been far too long. I trust thou art keeping well, Mercy?"

Mercy blanched. "Yes, I thank thee, Mother."

"And Grace? Hast thou got a cold on thy chest, Grace?"

"N-no, thank thee, Mother." Grace's fingers whitened with the effort of controlling her bodice.

"Er – Yes. Sister Unity tells me little Titty has caught the whooping cough. She seems to have been *most* unlucky on her last trip into Paradise." The awful smile slipped and was swiftly reinstated. "I am pleased that I find thee both well."

There was a silence while Mother Germaine pondered what to say next. She didn't want to *intimidate* the girls. . . . Perhaps a tactful reprise of what had led to the situation? Nonsense, it would only be foolish to waste time with that. Every member of the Society knew the situation – it was what they were to do about it that she had to explain.

How, exactly? The baffled breath whistled out softly between her teeth. "Oh, my. Grace. Mercy."

Mercy looked as though she were going to be executed.

"I am trying to find a way to tell thee why I called thee here. How to convey –" She paused. "– the great *honour* bestowed upon thee. Remember to be humble. I do not want thy heads turned." She nodded firmly. "Prepare thyselves. Pay close attention." A quick inspection: yes, their attention could not have been closer.

"We, the Eldresses, we, of the Hopeful Society of Faith in the Continual Resurrection, have selected *thee* to be our first missionaries." She sat back, waiting for the girls' reacfion.

There was none. Nothing happened. The girls didn't understand.

"Er –" She fumbled. "Thou art to go into the World –"

Suddenly, Mercy shrieked.

"– in order to make converts for our Society. Without fresh blood –"

Mercy shrieked again.

"– we all know the Society will perish. *Please*, Mercy, do *not* make that tiresome noise. Consider the honour conferred upon thee! The fact that we are entrusting to thee the Hopeful Society's fate. The opportunity to bring the Hopeful doctrine to the poor souls – Oh, my goodness! Grace, canst thou bring her round? I hope she hasn't bumped her head."

But Grace was sitting, staring, like a statue, with her hands still tightly clenched at her full bosom.

"Grace?" said Mother Germaine. "Grace? Canst thou hear me?"

"Did thou say –" Grace's voice was husky. "We are being let out?"

"Yes, child, yes. That is precisely what – Oh, for pity's sake move thyself and help me tend to Mercy!"

But Grace's mouth was the only thing about her that was moving. "We are being let out?" she husked again. "We are being let out?"

Mother Germaine had come round the table and was bending worriedly over Mercy. "Burning feathers?" she muttered. "Lorelei's smelling bottle? Come, come, child!" And she slapped at a handy, over-sensitive wrist. "Grace, for goodness *sake* –"

"Being let out!" Grace's eyes cleared, she let go of her bodice and jumped to her feet!

It was not what Mother Germaine would have desired as a cure for fainting, but bouncing bared breasts and wild screams of joy from her Hopeful Sister had a remarkable restorative effect in the case of Mercy.

In the twilight, when all was quiet, they sat and talked. At least Mother Germaine and Grace talked. Mercy moaned occasionally. The only interruption was when Sister Amy came in to light the lamps.

"So, then. It is understood, children." Mother Germaine blinked in the mellow brightness. "We must be bold – Philadelphia."

Grace said, "Oh, Mother, a city!" Beside her there was a wretched whimper.

"The best and the worst are always in cities. It is to be hoped thou wilt find the best."

"Grace'll be sure to find whatever's going." Amy, shielding her taper, was on her way out. She caught Mother Germaine's eye and added, "Sorry."

"*To be Hopeful is a state of mind. With God's help it may lead to a physical condition.*"

"Phrase thirty-seven," said Grace.

"Indeed, child. Thou wilt venture Hopefully into the World and our prayers will go with thee. As far as is possible, I will try to protect thee, and take all precautions lest thou feel too alone. Remember, we have time before thou leavest this blessed sanctuary. Thou shalt be prepared. Thou wilt be taught and advised in the ways of the World."

There was a happy sigh, and a feeble groan.

"I wish thou wouldst look on the positive side of this mission, Mercy. Thou mightest save not only the Hopefuls, but a soul for God. And couldst thou not blow thy nose? There, child, that's better. Tomorrow I shall take the buggy to Bird in Hand – someone will have to drive thee to the train station, when thou goest. It's not too soon to start making arrangements, and I can ask at the Plain and Fancy Dining Room. And I'll post a letter. Thou shouldst have decent, safe accommodation in the city. I'll write tonight."

"Where will we stay?" asked Grace.

"Thou shalt stay where I stayed, when I had to travel to Philadelphia. Oh, it was many years ago now." She made a self-conscious little gesture – a tug at the cap that sat snugly on her grey hair. "I had to go with Sister Florence – thou wouldst not recollect her, she was dead before thou wert born. It was to buy medical supplies, and goods at Wanamakers. We stayed at the Young Womens Christian Association, on Chestnut Street." Mother Germaine sighed nostalgically. "Those were giddy days. I hope and trust that this adventure will not alter thee, children. I beg thee never to forget the Phrasebook of Uplift."

"I know it by heart," Grace said. There was a sob from Mercy.

"That is good. Continue always to observe the customs of our Society. Read the Phrasebook at night, every night, for guidance, and remember to be Hopeful in the face of all temptation."

There was a respectful hush. Then Grace said, "And find converts?"

"Yes, dear child, and find converts."

"Male converts?"

"Yes, that's right, child, male converts."

"Men," said Grace blissfully.

Mercy whimpered.

"Oh, *men*."

Part Two

Babylon

IV

It was a man who drove them to Lancaster. A disappointingly old man, who didn't speak to them on the way. And they would have liked to speak to him, because this was the first time either of them had been in a horseless carriage, and they were nervous and excited. Their nerves and excitement took them differently: Grace scratched a lot, and Mercy cried. But she had been crying since early morning, when Mother Germaine had tried to make her put on The Clothes.

"They show my legs!" she'd wailed. "I don't want to wear them!" And she wouldn't. Apart from the half-hour she was so wrought up she stuck, and couldn't get them off.

Mother Germaine had explained over and over that this style of dress would be better for her, out in the World. But it was no good, Mercy didn't want her calves showing; and what was more, she had the Sisterhood on her side. Unity had flinched and said it was disgusting, Lorelei had squealed for spirits of ammonia, Heloise had disappeared in her apron, Amy had sat down and mended a stocking, little Titty had whooped and whooped in pure terror, and Agatha had said, "Mother! That skirt's nearly up to her *knees*!"

'Sister dear, I just wanted to make it easier for her – for *both* of them when they leave here. No-one in Philadelphia will be dressed as we are in the settlement." Mother Germaine had looked genuinely flustered. She had made a special trip to buy The Clothes in Paradise. "Everyone will stare at them in their Hopeful caps and long dresses. Surely thou dost not want the girls to draw attention – it has never been our habit to draw *attention* to ourselves."

But Mercy had her own logic: "I don't want my legs showing!" And rather than that a Hopeful missionary should be withheld by hysterics from the heathen, she had got what she wanted – covered legs – and that had been the end of that.

Grace had taken The Clothes, however, and packed them in Sister Agatha's loaned carpet bag. She would have been more sulky about not wearing her new dress if it hadn't been for Mother Germaine's words: if blue linen would get them stared at, she would happily stick to blue linen; besides, it went well with red hair. So she ungrudgingly chose not to look different from Mercy, and told the Sisters that she needed private practise to learn to cope with buttons anyway.

Buttons – and Mother Germaine had said *zippers*. It was going to be very different Out There. Doors that had locks and not latches. And houses with electricity.

And cars – did they all go this fast? Was going this fast compulsory? It made Grace feel very strange. The motion was so different from the buggy. The rich, green land rippled around them, the fields ebbed and flowed, the lush woods like carpets, the white farmhouses and fences, the old barns with the hex signs.

"Oooo-oo," sobbed Mercy. "I don't want to go!"

Grace would have liked to quote from the Phrasebook, but she thought she should save that for a crisis. If she started giving Uplift so quickly, they wouldn't have a Phrase left within twenty-four hours. She turned her head away from Mercy and stared through the window, at the enclosed black conveyances of the Amish people, at the goods being sold along the roadside, at the signs saying 'Pennsylvania Dutch Food' and 'Hexy Jake's Place'.

"Do look, thou should look, Mercy, there's so much going on."

"I don't want to see it! It's all too Worldly!"

"Oh, well." Grace slumped for a while, and then she sat up again and said, "There's another hex mark. Does thou know what that one means, Mercy?"

"Don't look at them, they're the work of the Devil!"

"They're very pretty, and they're supposed to keep out the Devil. Sister Unity told me they're against the evil eye."

The tearstained blonde moaned in anguish. "Thee *knows* they're the work of foreigners."

"They were only foreigners at first, when they came over. Everybody here was a foreigner at first." Grace pressed her nose to the window and muttered, "Even the Hopefuls."

She received a wail of misery in answer. "The Hopefuls were English women, and they believed in God! How can thee compare them? They didn't go about eating pretzels and putting those bold coloured things on the sides of barns. They believed in *goodness*, and *purity*, and *religion*. Grace, those people out there even paint tulips on *plates*!"

There was a muffled snort, which might have been a cough, from the driver in front of them. It was the first sound of any kind the driver had made. Grace was intrigued by it, but it did not stop Mercy.

"Those foreign people use pagan decoration! Sister Agatha told me their furniture's covered in curlicues!"

"Sister Unity told *me* it was a custom they brought with them."

Mercy sobbed. "It was a custom straight from the Pit."

The car braked for a crossing and Grace read out loud, from a wayside sign "'Come twist your pretzel'. I don't think there's anything very sinful about drawing flowers on a wardrobe." She reflected for a moment. "Aren't they just what Sister Unity calls the Gay Dutch?"

"Ooooruh! I won't listen to thee – thee'll be painting thy face next!"

Grace shrugged her blue linen and gave herself over to a study of the changing scene beyond the window. As time passed and the sky grew greyer and duller, and they approached Lancaster, Mercy's snivelling beside her increased. In truth (and Grace, swallowing, had silently to admit it) the outskirts of the town were not a sight to make anyone gladsome. Creeping up around them was an ugly, mis-shapen sprawl of featureless houses, idle gas stations and sullen blocks she decided must be factories. And overall an air of gloominess and low spirits, as though in Lancaster it were always and forever a day when women had bad heads and couldn't set their jellies.

"I don't like it! I want to go home!" wept Mercy.

Grace feverishly tried to find her a good thing. "Look," she said, and pointed. "Look, they have trees in the streets."

"Those trees are *sick*!" choked the weeper. "Can't thee see those poor trees are *dying*!"

* * *

In a redheaded resignation and a blonde wave of sobs they arrived at the station, and the driver, still taciturn, slewed the car to a stop and got out. When he'd worked the door handles for them, they got out after him, and faced a huge, red-brown building with white pillars above its entrance. It was the largest building either of them had ever seen, and carved in its stonework was the impressive word 'Pennsylvania'.

Mary stared, wailed and dived back in the car. It took the combined strength of Grace and the driver to drag her out again. She came feet first.

"Be brave, Mercy," Grace panted. "*No field is too large for the Hopeful plough*." And just in case the little blonde should take it into her head to dive off again, Grace weighted her down with the loaned carpet bag.

It was an uncertain procession that made its way through the gloomy portals: Grace, followed closely by Mercy, who was followed even more closely by the driver, who'd seen some distance up her under-skirts. The last of these three, issuing mute directions, kept poking Mercy in strange places with a pleased finger.

Up the steps they went, surrounded by brass and marble, and into a vast, shining and shadowy hall. Mercy's breath was a slobber and Grace eyed her sharply; if she bolted or fainted they'd miss the train to Philadelphia. But for the moment, at least, she appeared tractable, if whiney, and Grace rewarded her with "*To be Hopeful is a blessing. It is also necessary.*"

From the pocket which hung at her waist, the redhead carefully extracted the Amtrack tickets. Mother Germaine had obtained them, and that morning given them to her. It had been an awe-inspiring moment. With their money and the letter from the Young Women's Christian Association, confirming their double room, these vital slips had been consigned to Grace's care – not as the most reliable but as the least hysterical recipient.

It was a vital trust. She studied them, brooding over the figures, and as a precaution hooking her other hand through Mercy's sleeve. Then she put the tickets away again, said, "I thank thee very much" firmly to the driver, and propelled her blubbering companion towards the wide doors leading to the tracks. It was as well they had time, because their progress was slower than it might have been. Every few yards Mercy set down the carpet bag, and blew her nose, and whimpered, "I want to go home!"

Throughout the whole of the imposing building, which Grace had such frequent cause to stand still in, and observe, she only saw four masculine people. A man in a strange hat, who looked cross and suspicious. A woman in trousers, who had a backside bigger than Sister Amy's. And two little boys (and even they were by the sign that read 'Women').

It was not a suitable site, Grace decided, for starting to make conversions. Surely Philadelphia would prove a more Hopeful place.

V

The train swayed past the dismal grey houses, afloat in a worsening drizzle, and Grace held on tight to her pocket and chewed nervously at her bottom lip. She had known that Philadelphia would be a city. But that this was in fact what being a city meant – of that she'd had not the smallest idea. Rows of closed, dull-coloured houses, road-surfaces oily with rain, white paint daubs on the brick walls, disconsolate, ominous goods-yards, strange, towering mechanical structures, built to do who knew what things.

Mercy, worn out by crying, was dozing with her head on Grace's shoulder. Tears had left smeary traces on her rounded, golden-pink cheeks. Tendrils of blonde hair had crept on to her forehead. She looked so touchingly innocent that Grace wanted to scream. To be responsible for the tickets and money, to take care of herself in this thing called a city – all of that was, well, rather thrilling. It made her want to go to the water closet. But on top of all that, to have to take care of Mercy. . . .

She gave an exasperated wriggle and disturbed the sweet sleeper, who woke.

"Where are we, Grace dear?" mumbled Mercy, blinking.

"Thou knows as much as I do!" came the tart response. And then, seeing the stricken face, and grumpily relenting: "From the way those people are acting, we're nearly there."

Up and down the aisle, passengers were struggling into coats and reaching for luggage. Many of them stared fascinatedly at the girls.

"Put thy cap straight!" hissed Grace. "Thou can see thy reflection in the window." And she tugged at one of her own ringlets till it curled fetchingly around her neck. "Go on, Mercy. See, thou can make thyself pretty."

But Mercy was gaping at the dark glass and making little gurgling sounds. "Oh, the merciful Lord protect us! Grace, we've gone under the earth!"

Any passengers who hadn't been looking were attracted and began staring frankly now. And some of them weren't just staring, they were whispering. A black woman put on bright pink spectacles.

"Husssh!" This was not the sort of attention Grace had wanted them getting: people were gawking at them as though they were a couple of freaks. "It must be all right, Mercy, keep thy voice down. Nobody else seems worried. . . . It's only gone dark."

"Oooo, Grace, where's the *sky*? I don't like it, Grace, I'm frightened!"

Grace would not have acknowledged it for the World, but she was scared stiff. The window now was totally opaque and for ages they jolted along through a blanket of blackness, with Mercy's nails clutching and digging deeper and deeper in the flesh of her arm. Grace bit her lips and swore under her breath: it was agony. She would have told her to stop, there was blood on the linen, but it seemed such a pity if that kept her quiet.

At last when her arm was all holes the train began slowing, and through the pane she could make out dim light. Like lamps being carried through the fields on a foggy morning. Passengers hustled towards the doors. "Come on, Mercy, this is where we get out."

They wriggled into the aisle and nervously followed the crowd disembarking; on to the grim subterranean platform, and towards. . . . Mercy stopped dead as if struck by lightning, and quavered, "I'm not doing it!"

"Not doing what now, what aren't thou doing?"

Mercy went red and white. "I'm not going on that thing."

"*What* thing?"

"That shiny thing with all the people. Grace, they're going upstairs without moving their legs!"

Grace peered ahead and clenched at her pocket. Oh, if only for once righteous Mercy weren't right. The travellers were stepping on to a strange metal stairway and some invisible agency was hauling them all up out of sight.

"Perhaps it's a miracle," she croaked; it was difficult to sound certain. "Perhaps –"

"It's not a miracle! It's a work of the Devil!"

"The Devil, the Devil, it's always the Devil! How does thou know, Mercy? Does thou think God's stupid?"

"Oooo –"

"Why shouldn't God have made it for a change?"

She edged forward a short distance to inspect the weird engine, and when she turned back there was a wild look in her wide, golden-flecked eyes. "*And* there's no other way out of here."

"I don't care, I'm not –"

"Oh, yes, thou are!" Getting behind the failing Hopeful, Grace gave her an almighty shove along the platform. "Does thou want to stay underground for ever?"

"Nooo, but –"

"Thou's been the one always so scared of the Pit!"

They teetered at the foot of the stairs, Mercy fell on with the wrong boot, and it was only by using great presence of mind that Grace managed to snatch up the carpet bag. She staggered on to the engine in the wake of her blue-clad Sister, and so it was that shaking and flustered they erupted in the centre of Thirtieth Street Station. Eurydice must have been just as reassured by her first sight of Hades. There were people everywhere, and they all looked as though they wanted to be somewhere else.

"Oooo, Grace –"

"Hush now!"

Ranged round the walls of a huge, sickly-lit cavern were a line of glassed-over caves that their signs said were shops: Fannie May Candies, Pennsy Bargain Book Shop, Flower World and Pennsy Cosmetics Fountain.

"W-what's a c-cosmetics f-fountain?"

"How the Lord should I know?"

"Ooo, Grace –"

"Shut thy mouth!"

Dark recesses were labelled Rest Rooms, a bright squiggle read 'Soda Lunch'. Crowds milled like spilled wheat kernels and a man came up the engine behind the girls and said, "Geddout the way". Mercy said, "Oooo, I'm sorry!" and Grace said, "Get out the way thyself!" She also stood on his instep, which was a good move in solid laced boots.

The man's face went purple, which had upon the embattled redhead a quite amazingly pleasant effect.

She smoothed down her apron, ignored the strange foreign words the man was spluttering, murmured, "Over here, Mercy" and seizing her companion under the armpit, dragged her towards a central counter that bore the legend 'Information Desk'.

Two little gentlemen in shirt-sleeves were roaming around inside this pig pen, while above their heads the notices on a great big black board spun and flickered and clicked. Grace thought the shaky white letters were like Sister Agatha's teeth. Those large teeth were loose in their gums. Perhaps all the things in the World would turn out to be homely, if she stood firm and looked at them the right way up. She did not allow herself to wonder how in the name of the Lord the notices worked; that kind of pondering led to knock-knees, palpitations and behaving like Mercy, who had all the spunk of a chicken at the bottom of a pond. Grace raised her chin. *She* would not be like that. She was going to be brave, hold on to her pocket and crush as many insteps as possible. She was also going to have a good time. What did it matter if the black board chattered away all by itself, and reeled up crazy sentences when it had done skittering?

"One forty-nine. Metroliner. Washington. On time," she read.

There were rows of that stuff. The Phrasebook of Uplift was really thrilling in comparison.

"Pardon me," she said.

The shirt-sleeved men went on with their work. One of them, as he roamed, was reading an illustrated journal.

"Pardon *me*," she said.

"Ooo, Grace," whimpered Mercy.

The man with the journal glanced at her irritatedly. And stopped, riveted. His gaze whipped from Grace to Mercy, and back again. The look became a stare, his piggy little eyes widened, his grip on the shiny paper loosened and his journal fluttered and flapped, unfolding, to the floor. Grace leant over the counter to study the opened-out picture. It was of a plump, dark, and very sullen girl without her drawers on.

The man bent to pick up his property. Flushed in the face, he grunted, "You some kind of publicity stunt?"

"No. No, no, no." His friend in the pen had ambled to join him. "They're Amish. Can't you see, they're Amish."

"We are not Amish, we are Hopeful!" Grace retorted.

"*Hopeful*? Come on, you're Mennonites, aren't you? Mennonites with those little hats and the aprons?" The man without the journal made twirling motions in the air.

"We are not Amish and we are not Mennonites! We are members of the Hopeful Society of Faith in the Continual Resurrection, and we want to get to Suburban Station, please." Grace was conscious of Mercy, snivelling beside her. If only she had pulled her curls down out of her cap. She should at least be winsome, if she couldn't be firm and crush insteps. "Suburban Station's the nearest to the Young Women's Christian Association?"

Thus addressed, the man with the journal said, "How the Hell should I know?" The other man said, "Yeah, yeah, yeah. That's on Chestnut Street?"

"Please wait a minute." Grace rummaged in her pocket, and produced a paper. "Yes, that's right, it says on Chestnut Street. Mother Germaine said we have to go to Suburban Station, and we have to buy the local ticket here."

"Well, that's what you do." The friendlier of the two men smiled. His teeth weren't as white as his notices.

"Yes." Grace concentrated on looking Worldly. She tossed her head. But then she had to say, "Where do we buy the ticket?" and she had the feeling this spoiled the general effect.

"You see over there, where it says 'Ramp to Upper Level' – you go through that arch, there's a booth on your left, you buy your tickets and you go on up to the track." He smiled even more broadly; maybe his teeth didn't match his notices, but they certainly matched his black board.

"Thank thee." Grace nodded, to show she understood him. And she shook her Sister. "Come on, Mercy."

"I don't want –"

"Oh yes, thou does."

Travellers turned to watch as the girls marched through the station: Grace was doing the marching voluntarily; Mercy was forced. Their well-polished boots brought echoes from the stone flooring, and their long blue skirts swirled, caught and released between their moving legs. The carpet bag bounced. Currents of air from archways and doors stirred Grace's ringlets. Their blue caps bobbed, they exchanged hisses and whispers, and bent towards each other from tiny, supple waists. If Grace had known what the crackle of her starched apron did to the men she passed she would have been delighted; if Mercy had known what *her* crackle did, she'd have been terror-struck and mortified.

"That's it," said Grace. "Over there, opposite where it says 'Soft Pretzels'."

And they waited in line, behind two black boys with nice backs and a grey lady with very high heels and varicose veins. And Grace bought the tickets, and hustled Mercy farther along the ramp and on to the platform, and they stood hand in hand till the sleek, corrugated silver train came in.

VI

Chestnut Street, when they found it, was a very, very long street. Unfortunately they did not find it right away. First they found John F. Kennedy Boulevard, and then they found Arch Street, and then they found Cherry Street, and then they found out they were going in the wrong direction, and had been ever since John F. Kennedy Boulevard. Around about then the worst of the drizzle let up. By the time they had tramped block after block back down 16th Street the sidewalks were quite dry – but they weren't.

Grace stopped in a store doorway to wring out her apron, and muttered, "*No field is too large for the Hopeful plough.*"

"Thee keeps saying that, Grace. Grace, my boots are all wet."

"I know thy boots are all wet – does thou think mine aren't? And I keep saying that Phrase because I need it. If thou wants another one, I'll say another one." She took off her cap and wrung that out, viciously. "*A Hopeful woman carries the yoke through life and a Hopeful man carries the bridle.*"

Mercy stood biting her lips and dripping. "Th-that doesn't s-sound s-suitable, Grace."

Grace looked at her. It was the sort of look that could cure ham.

Ahead and behind them, Chestnut Street stretched, seemingly never-ending. They'd only just turned into it from 16th, and according to Mother Germaine's thumbed and sodden instructions, the Young Women's Christian Association could hardly be called near at hand. It wouldn't have been quite so bad if they hadn't gone wrong at the beginning, but Grace (who had been determined to be determined) had firmly held their map the wrong way up.

"Shake thyself!" she snapped damply at Mercy. "Thou's running like a gutter. Thy hems have dripped clear through Sister Agatha's carpet bag."

On the shop- and store-lined sidewalks, the crowds had reappeared with the end of the rainstorm; they peered in dark windows, they read café menus, they chewed comfortably on what they all had in their hands: Pretzel-links stuffed with mustard and frankfurter sausages. They paused to consider the bedraggled Hopefuls, and the redheaded half of the wet blue couple glowered hungrily back. She thought the chewing people looked like the cows back home on the settlement, only not so pretty, and if anybody should be stared at and gaped at and pointed at and mumbled about, *they* should. It wasn't as though there was little to see around, either. The stores were full of goods, the roadway was full of horseless carriages, and at short intervals along either side of the street there were groups of musicians – boys with almond eyes playing the fiddle and boys with braids playing the guitar. By a sign-post a pink girl was playing the cello, and on a corner a young man was doing rope tricks. Yet still the crowds stared at *them*, as though they were peculiar, just because they wore caps and aprons, and ankle-length skirts.

"Thou can do what thou likes," Grace hissed, savage, "I'm putting on The Clothes as soon as I get the chance."

Mercy stopped biting her lips and shaking her skirts and started a high-pitched wailing.

"Oh, hush! 'Show thy legs, show thy legs' – thou can show thy fanny for all I care!" And so saying Grace hoisted their sole piece of luggage and set off steamily for the Young Women's Christian Association. Five minutes later Mercy showed her first piece of initiative. She choked down her wails, wiped her face on her apron and ran after Grace.

Across 17th Street, 18th Street, 19th Street, they trudged, the colourful stores and the huge tall buildings becoming less and less frequent, the signs reading more and more often 'Discount'. There was a place called a Park but there wasn't a tree in it, just lots and lots of horseless carriages, and there was a block with a round verandah and big posters about adult entertainment, and that was really a motion-picture house. It wasn't until they'd dragged across 20th Street that Grace saw the letters 'YWCA' on the side of a porch up ahead of them; and Mercy got hiccups.

"Don't thee be – huck – cross, Grace. I can't – hup – help it. It's the – huck – excitement."

Grace gave her one look and she stopped hiccupping. She also went quite white with shock.

Perhaps, to be fair, it wasn't only Grace's look that blanched her. Perhaps it was the overpowering smell of bleach. Of such strength, so self-assured, that it had left the building to meet them, and overwhelmed them totally as they pushed their way through the smeary glass doors. Their throats, their noses, their eyes were seared and smarting; Mercy choked, "M-maybe they're doing their laundry?" But then she saw Grace's eyes (which matched her flaming hair) and said no more.

The two girls were standing, snuffling, in a shabby hallway. There was a rounded counter to their left and when they could breathe they stumbled towards that. Two black women in print dresses were sitting at desks behind the counter, having trouble with pencils and various large documents. Some emotion stirred them both briefly at the sight of the wet arrivals but then it vanished, never to return. One of them said "Yes?" to the girls, without getting out of her seat.

"We – we have a reservation." Grace coughed and dragged the soaked papers from her pocket. "We're from the Hopeful Society – it's beyond Lancaster?"

The woman who had spoken hauled herself to her feet and came over to the counter. Upon her, the bleach only seemed to have a slowing-down effect. She stood sorting through Grace's papers without actually looking at them. When enough time had passed she said, "The Residence Director'll wanna see you," and turned her back to handle a queer black device.

"Wh-what's *that*?" choked Mercy. "Oooo, Grace, she's talking to her*self*!"

"No, she isn't, doesn't thou remember what Mother Germaine told us?" Grace sneezed, and paused to cough up a lungful of bleach. "That's what they call a phonograph."

"Are thee sure?" Mercy was rubbing her sore, running eyes. "I remember about the motion pictures and I remember about the hot water coming straight out of the pump, but I don't remember about –"

"The Residence Director'll see you if you go on up. Third floor, take a right when you get out the elevator."

Elevator. The Hopefuls moved closer together. Mercy went "Aaaa-ccchooo!" Grace sneezed and coughed, and wheezed "Wh-where's the elevator?"

"Back there." The woman had returned to her desk and pointed, languidly.

"Th-thank thee." Coughing, Grace replaced her papers in her pocket. A certain lack of desire for the elevator caused her to linger. She managed, as casually as she could through the bleach, "Is th-this th-thy laundry day?"

The seated women looked at one-another. One raised her eyebrows and the other shook her head and closed her eyes.

"I m-mean the *s-smell*."

The woman who had been spared – who had not till now been dealing with the blue Hopefuls – spoke for the first time. She spoke loudly and clearly, as though to idiots. "Thass the chlorin' from the *swimmin'* pool."

* * *

In a dingy lobby with peeling paint was the elevator. But they didn't know how to use it, so they found the stairs. Remarks, hearts and names were scratched everywhere into the surfaces – on walls and even in one place scrawled on a ceiling – and on the landings there were notice boards where little notes signed 'Residence Director' were stuck up.

The light in the windowless corridors was harsh but lit nothing properly. It revealed the cracks in the plaster, but not the words on the little notices. It made the doors and the walls and the stairs bleakly crooked and oily, and it turned even rosy golden Mercy into a shadowy, greeny-grey corpse.

The climb to the third floor tired them, and they were already tired. Their damp clothing clung around them and hampered their climbing, and this time when Mercy wept, "I don't like it here!" Grace could think of nothing to reply. It took all her strength to drag one squelching boot after the other, and her thoughts ran exhaustingly from unpleasant rathole to rathole. The dark in her head seethed with questions, like what in the Lord's name a Residence Director was.

"I can't go any farther, I can't, I really can't!" wept Mercy.

"Thou doesn't have to go any farther, thank the Lord. We're here."

Or she hoped they were. They were facing a frosted-glass door that a fat girl was closing. The fat girl wore trousers and a tight upper garment and didn't appear to have on a camisole. She blinked at the Hopefuls and said, "Jesus Christ".

"Is this the Residence Director's office?" Grace's voice came out, she realised to her disgust, as feebly now as Mercy's.

"Yeah." The girl studied them both as they hesitated on the threshold. "Still raining, huh?"

"No." An attack of racked coughing. "It stopped almost as soon as we got wet."

* * *

The Residence Director was a tiny, wiry lady, whom Grace took for sure to be a tiny, wiry man. Then the talking began and Grace realised it was a female. All these trousers everywhere and the haircuts were so misleading. And she had never before met a lady who was quite like that – no bigger than Sister Lorelei, as earnest as Sister Unity, and not much older than either Mercy or herself.

This person sat on the edge of a chair and told them to sit down too, and they were to feel at home, they had a double room at thirty-nine dollars which was very lucky because there were only a few of those in the building, and what were their interests, and had they done any life-goal planning.

Grace and Mercy sat speechless, and dripped. Mercy, to Grace's fervent relief, had become too tired even to cry.

"Do you have career objectives?"

They gaped at her.

"What are your aims? Your *ambitions*?" The impassioned Director squinted at them. She was hugging herself round the knees.

Could they really tell her what their aims were in this city? Would she understand about converting men? In the Young Women's Christian Association? Grace stared at her pocket, frantic.

"You must have goals in life. What you want –"

"Oooo, *yes*!" burst out Mercy. She had shattering resources of lung-power, despite the exhaustion and bleach. "I do too want something! I do! Please, Ma'am , I want to be dry!"

VII

"Enjoy yourselves," droned the waitress, and she smiled absently, serving them Slimmer's Specials in Hollidays.

"She's always nice to us," whispered Mercy. "Can't we go home with her, Grace?"

Grace carefully counted through the money left in her pocket. Then she sighed. "If we don't start getting paid soon, we may have to."

They usually came to Hollidays around mid-day to look at the paper; it was just down the block from the YWCA. The Residence Director had said it was a diner, but they'd been pleased that whatever diner meant, Hollidays was also a café. And it was as cheap as cheap could be in Philadelphia, and it was clean and friendly; and when men followed them away from it they didn't have far to bolt.

The Residence Director had been full of advice, which turned out to be another way of saying life-goal planning. It had only distressed her that the girls were so 'unqualified' for any kind of 'career' work. A career was something you did for ever and ever, and with it went words like 'brassiere' and 'pension plans'.

Their ignorance of brassieres and pensions had gravely upset the Director. She had tapped her desk and talked about extended learning – motivation – training; asked whether the girls were into jogging, or took part in team sports. For all they knew, she could have been visited with the gift of Tongues. Her explanations and suggestions were painstaking, earnest and eager, and the Hopefuls listened but remained intrinsically Hopeful, and looked at each other out of the sides of their eyes. The Residence Director wrote herself firm, impressive little notes. But after a few interviews even she became noticeably lacklustre, and weakened to the point of suggesting domestic situations, which she recommended that they look for in the columns of the *Morning Inquirer*.

So the girls bought the newspaper each day and came to Hollidays to read it; and were served by a black waitress (who called them both 'dear' without discrimination); and sat eating whatever was cheapest on the menu; and squabbling but always eventually deciding that they didn't like the sound of *any* job the newspaper advertised.

They were nearing the end of their first whole long week in The World.

And what did they have to show the Society for all this experience? The gradual but frighteningly swift trickling away of their pocket money, a permanent strong scent of bleach and cold thighs when they wore The Clothes. The Clothes in The World had proved very draughty.

And despite the fact that they wore Them, people still stared – and stared hard, Grace had been the first to notice – though the staring now was more complimentary than otherwise. It was mostly masculine staring, too, which she thought was very nice.

It was sad and a shame that the kind of man who stared was not the kind of man, really, that was likely to be useful to the Hopeful settlement.

The whistles and husky remarks thrilled Grace to the bone (once she understood them), but whilst they pleased her hugely they only troubled and puzzled Mercy. And the redhead was very well aware that such remarks, whichever way thou took them, were no indication whatsoever of the temperament necessary for a convert. This did not mean she viewed the mutterers with Mercy's scared disapproval; it merely meant she knew they had more immediate ends in view than a pilgrimage to the Society out beyond Bird in Hand.

* * *

"We've got to do something, Mercy. We've got to stop being picky. *Hope is a lantern, take it out and raise it up* . . . To-day's our last day!"

"Thee means we're going back home to Mother Germaine?" Mercy was pink with joy, round her cottage cheese.

"No! I mean to-day's the last day before we run out of money. We have to find work – both of us, Mercy, yes, thou too. And it'll have to be where they'll give us something to eat." Grace began her usual frowning searching of the *Inquirer*. "If there's nothing in here I'm going to have to go to that hotel."

"Oh, no, thee can't, Grace. Mother Germaine can't ever have meant for thee to go walking in a place like that. Beatrice was in the kitchen last night when I was making our hot milk, and she said that hotel's Sodom."

Grace went on reading the paper. "I bet she didn't exactly say it like that."

"She said it plain enough, I knew her meaning!" The scrape of cutlery on a plate. "What's an air hostess?"

Grace's voice floated round the back page. "Did she say air or hair, Mercy? It might have to do with a beauty shop."

"Well, Beatrice says that hotel's full of them. She says all the men go there because of the air hostesses. She says the bar-room's like a cattle market."

"It sounds to me as though Beatrice talked her head off."

"Beatrice is lonely!"

"Beatrice borrows our supper."

"Beatrice is hungry!"

"Beatrice weighs two hundred pounds."

There was nothing but the rustle of paper, and Mercy sulkily swallowed her cottage cheese. She liked Beatrice, who was fat and friendly, and properly approached (told about the Society's Shoo Fly Pie, for instance) might one day become a Hopeful. They talked every night in the kitchen, while Grace stayed in her room and improved her knowledge of The World by reading glossy adult 'magazines'.

Their thoughts must have been running on the same subjects – Grace put down the newspaper and said, "Air hostess. . . . Air hostesses! There was a piece about them in one of those journals I was reading. Good Lord, Mercy, do they really stay there?"

"Stay where?"

"Oh, take that look off thy face, thou's not such a ninny. Stay in *that hotel*, of course!"

"Yes."

Grace's eyes sparkled. "They travel all over The World, Mercy, in heavier than air machines."

"Oh, my Heavens!"

"And they do things for men with some stuff called canapes. No wonder it's like a cattle market in the bar-room."

Mercy convulsed, scarlet over a radish. "Beatrice was right – thee can't go there!"

"Well, I don't know. . . ."

"No, thee can't, it's against all our teaching!"

"There's nothing in the Phrasebook about having to starve." Grace slammed down the *Inquirer* and started forking up lettuce. "Thou knows where I heard about it – from the Residence Director. She wouldn't sent anyone to Gomorrah *or* Sodom."

"Perhaps the Residence Director doesn't know about the air hostesses."

"Perhaps she doesn't." Grace chewed on some carrot. "How does Beatrice?"

"Some of the girls at the Association have worked there before."

"Oh, yes. And?"

"And they came back with fur coats."

Grace dropped her fork. "And thou's telling me not to work there?"

"Beatrice told me what they got the fur coats *for*."

Grace fell silent, except for the chewing. When she'd nearly finished, she said, "The Residence Director told me thou walks in and asks."

"No, Grace!"

"Thou just asks if they have a job, Mercy. She said I could get work as a maid."

"Ooooo –"

"I don't think that would be near the bar-room. *And* she told me I'd get a free coverall."

"What's *that*?"

"I don't know, but they'd give it to me." Grace cleared her plate. "I wouldn't have to do anything for it. Whatever it is, it can't be like a fur coat."

There was a violent blonde and pink and white eruption. "Well, I'm not working there!" Other customers looked round.

"Husssh!"

"I'm not selling my soul in that palace of sin!" Everyone started looking. "Mother Germaine wouldn't want me to go to perdition!"

"Shut thy mouth, Mercy, and eat thy carrot!"

"I don't want my carrot, I want to go home!"

Grace clenched her fists and hissed through her teeth: "If thou doesn't shut thy mouth I'll walk out and leave thee. Thou doesn't know how to pay at the cash-desk here yet!" Mercy shrank back. "Thou doesn't have the money and they'll put thee in prison. Or they'll make thee wash up until I come back!"

"Thee wouldn't do that, Grace!"

"Does thou want to bet?"

Mercy bent over her plate and desperately shovelled in carrot. She looked so frightened Grace was quite mollified. And after a few minutes, when nothing more happened, the other customers turned back to their own food.

The redhead waited, and from under her eyelashes looked all about her. Then she said softly:"I wouldn't expect thee to go and work in that hotel." The face opposite was lifted, and it was very tear-stained. "Oh, Mercy, thou does take everything so seriously."

Mercy gulped on her tears and her carrots. "Wha-what w-would I do then, wh-while thee w-was i-in th-that p-place?"

"Thou'd get a job as a maid in a nice house. With a family, Mercy, that would suit thee. That's what I'm looking for, and I'm sure I'll find it." She smiled soothingly and picked up the *Inquirer*, but seen through Mercy's blurred eyes, her expression was scary, and the way her lips curled was quite devillish.

She found Mercy a job in a house, though. A *nice* house, with pale-blue painted shutters, and steps up to a pale-blue painted door. It stood next to a house with dull-red painted shutters, that had steps up to a dull-red painted door, and there was an iron railing beside both sets of steps, and cobble-stones and lamp-posts on the sidewalk, and spindly, leafy trees in the narrow street. For a few short blocks around, all of the streets were like that. Cobble-stones and spindly trees and iron lamp-posts and even the same colours. It was a very easy place to get confused, and it was called Society Hill.

"Why's it called a hill when it isn't a hill?" whined Mercy.

Grace tossed her head. "That's none of thy business – perhaps they cut the hill off."

She was not in a mood to allow anyone to spoil things by whining. Having found the advertisement, she had been excited but hadn't at first known what to do. Then she had rushed to consult the Residence Director. The tiny wiry person had revived: yes, Society Hill could definitely be classified as a life-goal plan. There had been note writing. Society Hill was a place to be taken firmly. The Residence Director had made the telephone call for them, and talked to the lady of the house, and arranged an appointment for the following day, and actually sounded *humble*. Then she had told Grace how to catch a bus because it was twenty blocks away, and even the revived Director thought that might be a long walk.

"It's not," she had said chidingly, "as though you jogged."

And the Hopefuls had exchanged their usual uncomprehending Hopeful glances. And thanked her, very politely, very much.

It wasn't until a few hours later that they had found out, at last, what jogging was. Venturing forth for a celebratory soda, they had seen a girl in short underwear in the early evening in the main street, with everything she had bouncing up and down.

Beatrice had stood in the shared kitchen that night and explained that they'd seen jogging, and she had helped Grace put the cold towels on Mercy's head.

"If that's jogging," Mercy had mumbled, "it's the work of –"

"The Devil." Grace had grinned at Beatrice. "And if it is, Mercy, I think this time he's made a mistake."

So now, in possession of such Worldly facts, they stood on the steps of the nice house. They had washed and brushed their hair, and freshly laundered The Clothes. This had proved to be mixed in effect, because of The Shrinkage. Mercy was dressed in pale green, and Grace in pale lavender, and they had spent most of that morning sewing their buttons back on.

"My bodice is so tight I can't *breathe*, Grace."

"Well don't then," said Grace, and knocked the knocker, which rang a bell.

At this elegant turn of events, both girls were startled. Grace tried not to show it, but Mercy let out a shriek.

Lamps without wicks that lit up with switches, horseless carriages, running hot water, but not this. Where in The World were you when you knocked a knocker and it rang a bell? You were in Society Hill and you were standing on a doorstep, and a lady with stiff hair had opened the door and didn't like you.

"*Yes*," she said, as though she might bite them.

"We – we've – we've come to answer the advertisement." Grace grabbed Mercy, who was edging down the steps sideways. "The Residence Director telephoned about us – the YWCA Residence Director. We're from the Hopeful settlement."

"I only want one maid, why're there two of you?"

"I just came to see that my friend got here quite safe."

"O.K. you did, so goodbye." And an armslength of noisy bracelets reached out, swept Mercy in, and slammed the door.

Grace said, "Well, I don't know!" and sat down on the steps.

The woman stood in the close hallway, arms folded, scowling at Mercy. She was wearing a cream coloured shirt and trousers, she had a big pair of spectacles hanging from a gold chain round her neck and Mercy thought, tremblingly, that her face looked all wrong. Not just because she was scowling, although that was bad enough, merciful Heavens; but her nose was too narrow, her nostrils were pinched in, and she had no wrinkles. No laughter wrinkles, no bad-temper wrinkles – not even a tiny line. When she frowned, even Grace had tiny lines. But this woman's face looked as though it had been ironed with a flat-iron; it looked like a birthday cake with a smooth frosting. And Mercy had never, ever, seen a face like that.

"You'd better go in there," said the woman. When her mouth moved, her chin didn't. Neither did her silver-and-gold hair, when she jerked her head.

"In there" was a room off the hallway. It had a thick, shaggy, white rug on the floor and dark brown walls and many low tables. It was very full and did not smell of bleach. But it did smell of something – something funny. . . .

Mercy hesitated, uncertain, unable to enter, the woman with the stiff hair and the ironed face held up behind her and tsking impatiently.

And the woman smelled too! Her breath did, wafting around the Hopeful. What was it? And, oh, dear Heavens, Mercy recognised the smell.

Why, the room and the woman both *reeked* of poor, dead, dear Brother Orville's medicine. He was always taking it for his collitis, and the Sisters had found a whole bottle left behind in his room, after he had passed on. They had found a whole bottle that he'd left behind in the barn too. And in the woodshed, and in the privy, and in the pigstye. The settlement clanked with mementoes. Poor Brother Orville had never known where collitis might strike. It had struck him down in his bed, for weeks together. In the end it had struck him down off the roof. Could this be another soul suffering from the same illness? Thank goodness she didn't seem to be the type to risk fixing the shingles.

"Well!" snapped the women. "Go on in then!" And Mercy blundered forward, into the room. "You can sit over there." She pointed to a deep upholstered settle, and Mercy obediently sat in it and lost her backside. "That Director of yours said you were from some sect or other – what was it, Amish? – but she promised me you were clean."

"We're not Amish," whimpered Mercy, engulfed by the upholstery. "Grace told you, we're from the Hopeful Society, out beyond Lancaster."

"My God, *is* there anything out beyond Lancaster?" The woman gave a short, unpleasant laugh, as though nothing was funny, then she picked a water glass off a table and swallowed her drink. The drink tinkled. Perhaps it wasn't medicine; to Mercy it looked like iced tea. She and Grace had discovered iced tea quite quickly; it was cheap and they liked it, and there was more of it than there was of Tab, though that was altogether special because of low calories. Beatrice had explained all about calories one night in the kitchen, and now Mercy saw bread rolls and biscuits in a whole different light.

"So. You want a job here, in the big city. Have you got any aprons?"

"Y –"

"Never mind, I know what sort of aprons I want you to wear, we can forget those. Are you healthy? I don't want someone who gets a pulled back lifting a dust-cloth."

"Y – y – N – n –"

"I want this house well kept, we have a lot of guests and we give a lot of dinners and if there's one thing I can't stand it's a messy house. Can you iron?"

"Y –"

"I want full-time help, I'd expect you to take care of the things I don't send out." The woman went over to a tray and refilled her glass. Mercy saw that the iced tea came out of a bottle – just like Brother Orville's medicine. So she was ill. . . . The ironed throat moved, swallowing. Then she said "Have you got references?" and her voice sounded, *looser*, somehow.

But – references? Mercy quivered. "I – I don't understand, Ma'am."

"References. Letters from people you worked for."

"I never worked for anybody before, Ma'am. We've just come from the Hopeful Society."

The woman stood staring at her, expressionless. Not a line, not a wrinkle. Her fingers squeaked on her glass and she said "*Oh my God*."

Mercy blushed, deeply.

"Hopeful Society. You're not going to start preaching and praying and thumping the Bible instead of polishing the floors? You're not – what's it called, exclusive? You can eat *food*, can't you?"

"Oh, y –"

"Yes, of course you can eat. I never saw a maid yet that couldn't clean out the freezer." A slow gulp at the medicine. "There's something you'd better understand. It wouldn't do you any good *at all* if you started preaching. *Nobody* believes in God in this house. I believe in Valium and my husband believes in himself."

This time no attempt at an answer: the blonde girl was perching saucer eyed, and now she began stuffing her mouth with her thumb.

"I can give you a week's trial. That doesn't mean you go off and start growing your ego, the only thing that's right about you is the colour." The woman swallowed more of her drink. "It's my husband – I can't have black help because of my husband." She shrugged. "He isn't prejudiced, he just can't keep his hands off it." Another shrug. "Some men are like that. God, but when they made him they broke the mould. They just didn't break it soon enough." She looked through the bottom of her glass and said "C'mon, I'll show you round."

Mercy struggled out of the settle and nervously followed the cream-coloured figure up through the tall, narrow house. It wasn't really large, but it was complicated, and the air in it felt heavy, like a bolt of cloth.

On the same floor as the room they'd been in, there was another, even darker, with old purple rugs. Upstairs were 'our bedroom' – black and white with climbing plants and very hot – a green bathroom, a red bathroom, a blue bedroom which was for guests. Then came a study. "You don't go in there. Only my husband goes in there, you understand? You go in there, he'll kill you, doesn't matter what colour you are." Farther up still there were store rooms and "Your room, your bathroom. You don't use our bathroom, you use your own bathroom, always, you understand?"

"Please, Ma'am! You mean – I have to stay here at night?"

The woman frowned at her. "Sure you stay here at night. What happens, d'you turn into a pumpkin? You stay here, you stay here at night, period. I don't like the clearing away left till the morning. I don't like that *atmosphere* that gets around in a house after a party. God, I hate that atmosphere." She turned away from Mercy, reached for the bannister, swaying slightly, and made her way cautiously back downstairs. On the lower floors, at the basement level below the hallway, were a kitchen, a laundry area, cellar and storage space.

The smooth cream lady stood in the middle of the kitchen, propped against the wrought iron holder of some pans and a plant arrangement. She had poured herself more medicine, from a bottle she had taken out of a cupboard. "Y'know how to handle a dishwasher?"

"No, Ma'am. I never had to give anybody orders."

"*Oh Christ.*"

Mercy blushed for the Hopeless soul, and looked around, marvelling. She recognised the sink; she recognised the top of a stove; she recognised a few of the knobs and switches they had at the Young Womens Christian Association; beyond that she didn't recognise anything.

"You *can* use a vacuum cleaner." The woman peered at her from beneath newly lowered eyelids. "Oh no. Oh *God*. Don't tell me you can't – O.K. you can't use a vacuum cleaner. What did you do – where was it? – out beyond *Lancaster*?"

"Ma'am?"

"*What did you do when you wanted to clean the floors*?"

"We swept the floors, Ma'am, with brooms and brushes. In the kitchens and the still rooms, we scrubbed."

"You scrub floors here and I'll tear your ears off."

"Ooooo –"

"*This* is genuine parquet." The woman lifted her glass, puzzled. "Where'd I put that? You come on Monday morning, nine o'clock, you understand? I have to get up that morning, anyway. Mondays I meditate. One week's trial, you break anything and I'll take it out your wages, don't be late and stay healthy – I can't stand sick people."

She helped herself around the work tops, out of the kitchen by holding on to the cupboards, up the stairs, along the walls, through the hall.

"Well –" She fumbled open the door. "G'bye."

The pretty painted door crashed shut, and Mercy stood at the top of the dainty stone steps. She put out a hand anxiously to the railing. And snatched it back. Where was Grace?

And Grace, at that moment, appeared running towards her round the corner. She was wiping her mouth with the back of her hand, but there was a blob of something on her nose, and the something was green.

"Does thou know there's *pistachio* ice-cream, Mercy! It's green and it's the most wonderful taste in The World, and I've been in an ice-cream parlour called 'Once Upon A Porch'!" Grace leant against the house, panting. "What happened? Does thou like the place? Did thou get the work, Mercy?"

Mercy looked down at Grace's green nose, which went well with red hair, if not with The lavender Clothes, and said dolefully, "Yes, I suppose I did."

"But that's all right then. Why does thou look so sad? What's the matter, Mercy?"

"Don't thee scold me, I do feel so sad and I can't help it." Mercy seized hold of her skirt and only just remembered in time that she shouldn't lift it up to wipe her eyes. "Grace, that poor woman in there has to take the same medicine as Brother Orville!" She wrung her skirt and wailed, "Grace, that poor woman in there must be dying!"

Grace responded. A knot of little lines gathered between her slender, arching eyebrows. Her green nose twitched. The corners of her mouth wriggled violently, almost as though she wanted to laugh but wouldn't. She stepped up and patted her Sister comfortingly on the shoulder. "Never mind," she soothed. "Now thou has a mission in thy life, Mercy. Thou can make that poor woman's last days on this earth happy and Hopeful. How much is she paying thee?"

"I don't know, I never thought to ask."

"Oh, Mercy!"

"Don't thee be cross, Grace, how can I take money from a dying woman!"

"Phrase forty-four." The redhead licked her lips; her pink tongue flicked up and touched her pretty nose, piously. "*Never refuse money, it can always be washed.*"

VIII

So could a neck be washed, and it was, at least twice too, before Grace set out that afternoon for the hotel. Whatever they wanted, hers would be clean.

She left Mercy in their room with the Phrasebook and an apple, and escaped from the chlorinated YW into the warm and sunlit streets.

Spring had come. Each day in The World had brought finer, drier weather, and she did not hurry over much, but looked in the windows and strolled.

Grace liked Chestnut Street better, the nearer she came to the elegant stores and cafés. She admired the people now, with their mouths always full of soft pretzels on the way to their stomachs, and she paused happily to listen to the fiddling, fingering musicians, and she was stared at by men (which, though no longer a new thing, was still gratifying), and the only little black pinch in her mind was the state of her Dress.

She could feel the tightness of The Shrunk Clothes under her arms, and the rubbing where the seams cut into her armpits and cinched at her waist, making her sweat. From time to time a surreptitious glance down reassured her that the front was holding itself together, but there were great, bursting distances between the buttons in their straining buttonholes. A Phrase bothered her: *Hopeful Sisters, carefully tend to thy clothing. The Devil waits in a slack fastening.* But how was she supposed to tend to her clothing – this wasn't the Society's strong, serviceable blue linen. This was thin cotton, and when it had strunk it had also faded; she was probably lucky it had not fallen quite to pieces. Grace sighed philosophically – and couldn't help noticing reflected in a nearby window the remarkable effect her sigh had upon both The Clothes and the passers-by. Her philosophical mood became one of optimism. Really, it was so uplifting how out of evil could come forth a bit of good.

She turned the corner into bustling Seventeenth Street; with every step the sidewalks were becoming more interesting, noisier, more brotherly and more crowded. She allowed herself a juicy tremble of excitement – Philadelphia was a big city, what would the hotel be like? She had never been in an hotel, although she'd heard all about them. People stayed in them, and had food and baths. The Residence Director had said this was a good one, she had fascinated Grace with it, and nothing Grace had heard from either Mercy or Beatrice had caused her to alter her mind.

She halted at a kerb with the other people and patiently read the bright red "Don't Walk" sign. She read it for several minutes, across the roofs of the horseless carriages, and then she read the sign when it went green and said "Walk". So near now! She skittered across the roadway, turned another corner, ran under the nose of a horse that was carrying a rather cross looking policeman, hurried over some paving, trod on to a mat and was sucked into the dark, velvety lobby of her destination.

There were places to sit everywhere, and city people sitting in them. And nobody she could see was wearing a Dress anything like what she had on. Not even anything like what she'd had on before it shrunk.

Most of the ladies were very wide across the hips and the bosoms, and had square, high-coloured bodices, and trousers that stopped short and showed their swollen ankles. They sat about in dark spectacles, turning their heads creakingly and calling to one-another – things like "My God, my feet Ethel!" and "Just another Martini".

There were young women too, in smooth, rippling skirts, who weren't sitting but stamped through the lobby, and men in big check jackets who looked tired, and men in dark suits who looked very wide awake.

Grace stood hesitating, held up in the soft rug, and then Hopefully approached the nearest desk. Three young men behind it were having a conversation.

One of them said, "I *know* it was three oh five."

Another said, "Well, it's news to *me*! But nobody tells me *anything*!"

The third stood silent, shuffling pieces of card.

Grace put on a winning smile, and cooed, "Pardon me?"

The young man with the cards came over and said, "Yes, Ma'am." Behind him a voice said, "I *know* it was three oh five."

"Could thou please tell me if thou has any work for maids, please?"

There was a terrible silence. Grace realised that. She understood straight away that it was not a friendly but a terrible silence. Then the other two young men flung themselves over. One of them had bulging eyes: "You don't come into the lobby looking for work, you use the service entrance!" The other moaned, "Dear *God*, if I get through another day –"

The young man with the cards was the calmest. He only went white and shouted at her. But he said he'd ring the Personnel Manager, at least that was what Grace thought he said, and he directed her outside and round the block to the service entrance, and he said she'd be met and would she go now.

Which was how she came to be sitting in a fuggy office, in a corner at the back of the hotel, right next to a desk where a brown-haired girl with spots all over her face sat eating candy and rolling paper into a type-writing machine.

Grace enjoyed watching her – she was almost as good as a naked savage.

The girl would put a piece of candy in her mouth, squirm around on her chair till she was comfortable, and then begin patting on the flat little buttons of the machine. It made a very loud clacking noise, and a banging, and every so often it made a ping, and very often the girl would say, "Oh, shit!" or "Shit, shit, shit!" and lean on her elbows and feed other tiny bits of paper into it. She would fiddle around and peck at the buttons, and at last she would sit back again and put more candy in her mouth, and begin patting away until she cried, "Oh, shit!" (or "Shit, shit, shit!") and the ceremony was repeated.

Grace could have watched her for hours.

But it was only forty minutes by the wall-clock before a buzzing sound came out of a box on the desk and a harsh voice squawked, "Come in!"

"That's you," said the girl with the spots, without stopping her patting. "Oh, shit, shit, shit!" And Grace got up, and checked her Clothes front, and went on in.

A man was sitting behind a big desk, reading over some papers. He didn't look up, he didn't say anything, so Grace posed, waiting. She saw that he had combed his hair very carefully across the top of his head, where the pink skin showed flaked and scaly, and the hair was greased to keep it in place covering him, and he had pudgy hands and polished fingernails. When he finally looked up, she saw too that he was fat and pale and shiny, and the expression which had been on his face for studying his papers altered as he got his head lifted and was quite changed by the time he was looking at Grace.

His eyebrows had been drawn down, and now they rose up his forehead like window blinds. There had been a deep fold at the top of his nose, and it smoothed clear away. His lips had been pressed together, and they spread round his face. He had a dimple in his chin, but that didn't change.

"Uummmm, nowwww . . ." he said. "And what can we do for you?"

"Please, sir, I'd like to get work as a maid." And Grace, because she knew it was fetching, gave him a little curtsey. She had practised this in the bathroom at the YW, and had needed to because she hadn't curtseyed since she first got the curse. Hopefuls didn't expect girls to curtsey after puberty. But she knew it would give him a chance to take a look at her strained buttons, she knew watching her move in The Clothes was, for men, very pleasing, she knew just what her eyes were like when she glanced up from under her eyelashes, and she did all of these things because she wanted the work.

"Phrase thirteen," she had said to herself, curtseying diligently in the bathroom. "*The Hopefuls shall inherit all that the meek leave over.*"

The Personal Manager got up, and breathed loudly, and closed the door. Then he straightened his tie, and brushed down his jacket, and sat on the edge of his desk, and asked whether she was experienced. And then he seemed to decide that that didn't matter, and he was very nice above her coverall, and he told her to tell the Housekeeper she was a size twelve, because she didn't know what size she was, and he measured her so he could *tell* her what size she was, and they had a very nice talk and he sweated an awful lot. He put his fat hands on her and he asked huskily if she liked that, and she thought a long time and said she wasn't sure. Then he took *her* hands and put them on *him* and asked breathlessly if she liked *that*, and she said it was very interesting.

They had to stop this game because the girl with the spots knocked on the glass door, and the Personal Manager went back behind his desk, hobbling, and he had a very red face now instead of a very pale one, but Grace smiled at him and beamed at him and gave him another curtsey and little drops of saliva ran out of the sides of his mouth.

So then he said she was to report for work Monday, and she should collect her coverall and her cleaning trolley from the Housekeeper, and the Housekeeper would tell her all her duties, and he said "Social Security Card" but Grace didn't have one, and she wrung out a tear or two about that so he said he would *get* one, as though it were something big, like a pig-pen, and he said a hundred and fifty dollars a week and when the spotty girl had gone his voice became very strange again, and he put his hands on Grace's behind before she went out. Grace wouldn't have minded at all, except he had sweaty palms.

Part Three

The Road to Damascus

IX

Mercy was cowering in a corner of the kitchen, watching the blender and the dish-washer do their worst. She had covered her ears to keep out some of the racket, she was almost entirely sure she had put the cake-forks in the wrong place, and she really was about as miserable as she had ever been in her whole life.

She had been working for Mrs Hiscock Mincham Muschamp of Society Hill for a very long month (the death was obviously not going to be sudden), and the highlight of her days was the half-hour each afternoon when the lady of the house sent her out to stay healthy and she could walk down to Front Street and sob heart-brokenly in the Delaware.

She only met Grace on her days off (if she was lucky and they both had the same free time), and their main recreation was to take rides on the Fairmount Park trolley and sit talking and being thrown around and being winked at till Mercy was too overcome and they had to get off.

Grace had lately, Mercy had noted with horror, begun using lip-rouge. She had also purchased a selection of more Worldly dresses, and had one day shocked Mercy right to the Hopeful marrow by revealing she now wore coloured underwear. *And* it wasn't cotton, it was artificial. What had become of the Society's teaching, and its white linen drawers? Mercy's fears for the future of Grace's immortal soul were multiplied.

Grace only talked of aerosol polish, drip-dry and shopping. She was ecstatic, having convinced the Residence Director that she needed a lot of space to hang up The Clothes – and therefore still required at least a double room.

She told Mercy that keeping the double room was A Precaution.

Mercy took the Phrasebook of Uplift to bed with her every night. From Society Hill she wrote Mother Germaine long and pitiful letters, and posted them in night-safes and trash-bins.

When it came to converts, neither of the girls could report success in their mission. Grace merely looked shifty whenever Mercy wept over the subject, and Mercy herself rarely met anybody, because she spent most of her time when guests came hiding in the kitchen. She had been found there, after a week, by the ironed lady's husband, Dr Hiscock Mincham Muschamp, who pressed her up against the refrigerator and told her he was a proctologist.

This had caused poor Mercy terrible agonies of conscience; would Mother Germaine have wanted her to work for a Catholic? But Grace went and looked the word up in a book-store, and said as long as Mercy didn't turn her back on him she'd be all right.

They were amassing, Mercy was distressed to see, an astonishing quantity of filthy lucre. But what they were not amassing was clean, Hopeful souls.

* * *

Mercy peered at the clock, and went and switched off the blender. It was almost time to wake the sleeping Mrs Hiscock Mincham Muschamp with her celery and carrot juice. The lady lived on her medicine, cracked ice and raw vegetables, but she could only get the vegetables down liquidised.

Mercy spent many hours on her knees for Mrs Hiscock Mincham Muschamp, way above and beyond the call of polishing. Every time the ironed lady slammed into the house screaming, "That Goddammed car's stalled again!" Mercy knew this cry would be followed by the clashing of bottles. Mrs Hiscock Mincham Muschamp's condition was not helped by what she called her Mercedes.

Nor was it helped by the various committees. She lived on those, too, as well as the celery and carrot juice. She devoted all her strength to dressing and having her hair made stiff for them, and would return in the evenings on the verge of unpinned hysteria.

There would be splashing sounds and chinking and ranting, and orders to clean the tops of the doors – "Goddammit they're filthy!" – and the information that that bitch Mrs Routledge Barron Gibson Harrap Cambridge had got herself elected by donating a Picasso lithograph.

Today was a Friday. Not a good day, because Dr Hiscock Mincham Muschamp would be coming home for the weekend, and he and the lady would have more than forty-eight hours to bicker and chew ice-cubes at each-other, instead of less than three.

Worse than that, it was the start of an especially social weekend, and one whose meaning Mercy could not quite understand. Tonight was something for men called The Copper Beeches, and Dr Hiscock Mincham Muschamp was going to it (perhaps to talk about trees?), and someone he knew was coming all the way down from New York State to go to it with him. Mrs Hiscock Mincham Muschamp had been chewing ice for weeks. And every time she chewed ice or drank her medicine or screamed at her husband, he would swing away into his study with the *Evening Bulletin* and the salted almonds. And later, from inside his study, there would be mutters and talking, and all of the talking would be in peculiar accents, as though he had a whole lot of foreigners in there.

Mercy had shaken like an ague victim the first time this happened: the Devil and the fallen angels had brought Hell to Society Hill.

But the ironed lady had been in the mood to make herself an ally, and had spent an increasingly slurred four hours explaining video cassettes. The proctologist, apparently, watched and listened to these engines for consolation, and emerged from his study emotionally, if not spiritually, cleansed.

Tomorrow evening was The Masters Class, for men and women, to which Dr *and* Mrs Hiscock Mincham Muschamp were going, with the man friend.

On Sunday there was a brunch, whatever that was (although Mrs Hiscock Mincham Muschamp had said it would be fattening), and the lady and her husband would be having to leave that early, because they were driving to the shore to look at properties. A property was not like their house in Atlantic City; a property was having a house in Long Beach Island. And this expedition to look around at properties was so important that for the ironed lady it was the most important part of the weekend. When Dr Hiscock Mincham Muschamp had said, "But what about Jackson?" Mrs Hiscock Mincham Muschamp had shrieked, "I don't give a shit!"

So whilst the names and times of these activities floated in the ether, and were bandied about above Mercy's blonde, angelic head, she heard but did not fully understand their meaning. To her they were understood in terms of cracked ice and the kitchen. They meant that only Mrs Hiscock Mincham Muschamp would be in for dinner this evening (medicine and the blender), that no-one would be in for dinner tomorrow evening, that no-one would be in for either aspirins or lunch on Sunday, but that she must get back early from her afternoon off in case Jackson wanted a meal.

Pouring the thick juice into a tall glass beaker, she shuddered at the thought of what this gentleman 'Jackson' might be like. Most of the Hiscock Mincham Muschamp friends were noisy, and ended their visits being very ill in all of the bathrooms. Mercy had quickly learned to lock her door and put a chair under the handle; otherwise the friends came in and fell down heavily, or tried on her Clothes. On one occasion two of the friends had curled up in her bed while she was still in it, but luckily they had fallen asleep immediately.

She put the beaker on a tray, together with a little cloth and a vase holding a rosebud. She always felt a certain terror when she did these things. She did them because Mrs Hiscock Mincham Muschamp always insisted, but there had been a day when the ironed lady had roused from a stupor, reached out blindly and swallowed, and gagged horribly on the rose.

The tray, however, did look just as Mrs Hiscock Mincham Muschamp would have wished it, and Mercy pulled herself together and carried it from the kitchen and through the hall. She was putting one little foot on to the first stair when there was a ring at the door-knocker.

This was one of those complicated moments she dreaded; it wasn't possible to answer the door carrying things – there were rules. She had to hurry back to the kitchen and leave the tray there, and all the time the lady would be lying upstairs getting more cross, because she would have woken and been able to hear that Mercy hadn't answered the door.

The knocker was ringing again by the time she had scuttled back and forth and smoothed her apron. She was dressed in dull-grey and white, which went perfectly with the house. It was also the dreariest colour-scheme that could be found for her, and to Mrs Hiscock Mincham Muschamp's bitter chagrin it did not wash out her maid's pink and gold impact one bit.

Mercy took a deep breath, closed her eyes and prayed, and unfastened the latches.

"Good afternoon," she said, and "Good afternoon," said the grey-haired, portly gentleman standing on the doorstep. He bowed at Mercy, and he smiled, and his smile was very kindly. Anyone in The World would have told her it was also incredulously lecherous.

"S – sir?"

The grey-haired gentleman bowed again. "My name's Jackson." Then he looked less cheerful and said, "They tell me I'm expected."

"Oooo, yes, indeed thee are, sir. Please come in."

Mercy held the door open wide, but because of the narrowness of the hallway Jackson still had to brush against her to get past. She smelled of fresh soap, there was a crackle in her apron, she was flustered, with anxious smiles and little quiverings, and the gentleman took a very long time to come inside the house.

A voice which Mrs Hiscock Mincham Muschamp used for her visitors came floating like a seraph down the stairs. "Merrrccy, deeerrr, was that someone at the door?"

"Yes, Ma'am!"

"It's only me, Cordelia."

"*Jack*son! Oh, *God*, what *will* you be thinking of me? I should have been down to meet you – Kegan'll kill me. But I've been lying here with one of my heads –"

"Better than having to lie there with the two of them."

There was a deathly silence from upstairs. Then there came distinctly the sound of medicine. A piercing squeal announced, "Mercy'll show you to your room!" and a door banged.

Mercy looked agonisedly at Jackson. Jackson looked complacently at Mercy. "Cordelia," he said, "could never be accused of having a sense of humour. Not about herself, anyway."

Then he said "Hello, you know me, I'm Jackson. And how are you – Mercy? Did anyone ever pester you about being called Mercy? Mercy on us, and all of that – no?"

Mercy shook her head, but she was shaking all over. None of the Hiscock Mincham Muschamps' visitors had ever really spoken to her before.

This one had long grey eyelashes, and grey eyes with lots of folds at the corners; she couldn't help seeing because he was standing right up so very close to her. There was only his stomach keeping them apart.

"Well – are you going to show me to my room, Mercy, or would you rather die of fright in the hall here?"

"N-no, sir. Y-yes, sir, I'm sorry. I'm sorry." Mercy flushed down her neck. "It's this way." She reached round him for the bag he'd set on the hall floor, but he stopped her, and said "No! Thanks, I can manage. I'm not quite at the age when young girls have to carry my bags."

He talked to her, climbing the stairs behind her. "Mercy . . . You happy here, Mercy?" She heard him puffing – perhaps the bag was heavier than he'd thought. "I'll bet Kegan's happy – do you have trouble with Kegan?"

"Sir?"

"Kegan Muschamp. Kegan Muschamp!" He reached the landing and held the bannister, gulping in air. "That's who he was before he started commemorating dead people." Huff – gasp. "Hiscock Mincham – Hiscock . . ." Mumble. He scowled at the master bedroom. "When I think that poor –" Mumbles. "– a cousin of mine.'

Mercy kept silent throughout this, partly because she did not know what he meant. And partly because she did not know how to comment; the Hiscock Mincham Muschamps paid her wages.

She led Jackson nervously to the guest room, showed him his bathroom, and his towels, and his soap-on-a-rope, and then asked him if there was anything else he needed.

Jackson sank down on the bed and looked at her and said, "How old are you, Mercy?"

"Eighteen, sir. N-nearly. I think – I'm not sure exactly."

"Eighteen, uh? Eighteen. . . . If I told you what I needed you'd leave the house. Could you get me some tea, do you think?"

"Oh, y-yes, of course, sir."

"Then perhaps you'd better."

And Jackson observed her as she left the room, blushing, and he sighed and shook his head ruefully, and later in the bathroom mirror he had a friendly talk with himself. It was a habit he'd got into, since his wife had left him. "Now get your mind off it, Jackson," he said, "and just shut your mouth. Eighteen. *Eighteen*, for God's sake! Oh, Christ, what it is to be a dirty old man."

For Jackson was fifty-seven years old, five feet seven inches tall, and much too heavy for that height to please his doctor, lonely, humorous but lacking an audience who appreciated his humour, impotent since his wife had left, and quite desperate.

X

The meeting of The Sons of the Copper Beeches had gone as it had always gone – it was unthinkable it should have gone otherwise. The members had gathered at the Orpheus Club, there had been the cocktail hour, the toasts (first toast to Holmes, second toast to Watson, a toast to "the Woman"), followed by dinner upstairs in the large old room, walls covered by photographs of dead and alive members, and Jackson had glued his mind to the proceedings and unglued it from what Mercy might look like wearing only the apron of her uniform.

It was his harmless, escapist, abiding pleasure to be a Sherlockian. A Sherlock Holmes buff – a devotee. An interest he had walled himself up in when his wife had slammed out of Pleasant Valley. He had, of course, been a Sherlockian since he could remember – without realising for very many years that there was such a thing, or what a Sherlockian was. Sylvia had been driven insane by it – "Jackson, I will not have that filthy old hat in my house!" when he had procured from somewhere a deerstalker and placed it with pride and pipes on his mantelpiece; and, when he had acquired an early edition from England, "Jackson, that thing'll give us erysipelas!"

But Jackson had read the stories with pleasure since childhood, and Sherlock Holmes had repaid the hours of scholarship with compound interest. He and Watson had materialised in the form of a ticket out of IBM. Jackson had written a book on Sherlock Holmes – at nights, while Sylvia was in bed with a bowl of chocolate chip or fudge ripple and the television. He had begun it as an affectionate spoof, as a laugh, he had enjoyed what he was doing immensely – and the book had been immediately accepted, and when he was fifty-two had changed his life.

He became an invested member of the Baker Street Irregulars, a literary figure, a full-time writer, taking advantage of a window programme and leaving his job with four years guaranteed half-pay.

And Sylvia had said, "It's that hat or me!" and had left him.

He wrote a great deal, he read a great deal, he would have drunk a great deal but it affected his ulcer, and here he was sitting in the venerable upstairs room of the Orpheus Club, surrounded by the conservative fellows who formed The Sons of the Copper Beeches – the one-hundred-and-twenty-year-old scion society of Sherlockians in Philadelphia. . . . And he could not stop thinking about a rounded little pink and gold blonde who wore no make-up and was obviously scared half to death.

He had asked Kegan about her, and Kegan had said she was Amish or something – waved vaguely and said she was simple-minded, didn't like using machines, and called people "thee", but "Cordelia thinks in our position we should have her."

Jackson thought in his position *he* should have her. If he could summon up anything to have her with. For all too long he had been attached to a length of limp spaghetti – the equipment had not been in the sort of shape he could share around. Yet today in the hall he had felt physical stirrings – stirrings of a kind he hadn't felt for five years now, except in a few solitary pornography-inspired fantasies.

Mercy. . . . He fixed his mind on a cruet. He was fifty-seven years old, he told himself, with a weight problem. Impotent. . . . He knew his limitations.

Later he drove Kegan home (he thought he'd better) and they found Cordelia waiting up for them. It was Cordelia's habit to wait up for anyone home-coming, in a prone position with a glass on the drawing room couch. Kegan removed her glass, and she threw an ashtray at him, and it took the two of them to help her noisily to bed.

Jackson went and lay on his own bed, in his room, and wondered how far up in the house Mercy was sleeping, and that night for the first time since his twenties he had a quite incredible wet dream.

The following day broke with fresh exigencies: Jackson, his control strained to the limit, was energised to have Mercy bring him his breakfast in bed. She set the tray down, and said, "Is that all right, sir?" and Jackson, whose large lap was affected, said, "Yes thanks, very kind of you, Mercy" in a voice that even a mother would have thought strange.

At noon Cordelia disappeared to have her hair manoeuvred, and Kegan unlocked his study to show Jackson his latest acquisitions – more prize volumes wrested from antiquarian booksellers, an of-the-period magnifying glass, a hypodermic, a new pipe or two. Cinema posters of the early Sherlock Holmes films, a framed photograph of a meeting of the Baker Street Irregulars, who all (Jackson suddenly realised) had either been surprised by the flash-gun or were just naturally wall-eyed. Sherlock Holmes was the only interest Kegan and he had in common; Jackson sometimes wondered which of them was reading between the lines.

The day sweltered on – it was May in Philadelphia. And Jackson longed for his own cool, tree-shaded, Pleasant Valley N. Y. garden, instead of these niminy-piminy dusty little paved streets.

At the Masters Class meeting that evening, there were women – many of them young and some attractive. But Jackson felt the old accustomed insulation. There was no hot pinching twinge of reflex to them, the stirrings with Mercy must have been a freak remission, and he stood about watching everybody else get drunk. The Masters Class had only been running for a few years: a pre-menopausal, co-ed, Holmes splinter group. It was very hot, with thunder in the air, and Jackson thought about Mercy – alone in the house now – and whether she'd be scared of the thunder. Sylvia used to get her best orgasms during thunder-storms.

For his hostess the Saturday night was no better than the Friday, Cordelia managing only to remain vertical and intelligible until she was in the back seat. She had a terrible fight with Kegan all the way home and throughout the early hours of the morning, centring mainly on the amount he had given to a so-called literary agent to tidy-up a book *he*'d – hah! – written on Sherlock Homes.

Jackson drowned his smiles in his night-cap Bourbon. This was the first he'd heard that Kegan could write more than cheques. That night he didn't sleep much, but he read late, and out of each page rose rosy Mercy, gold and nubile, and called him "thee" and wore her apron and garters.

The Brunch on Sunday was OK if you weren't hung-over, but practically all those Sherlockians who attended it were. It was held outdoors in the azaleas until the storm broke, and the Hiscock Mincham Muschamps, by general agreement, and despite their lack of deserving it, had quite the best of it. With a good excuse they drove away in a high-tide of water, whilst everyone else was packed against the tightly closed French windows, wringing out hot muffins and scrambled egg.

Jackson, given a lift back that afternoon by a Sherlockian from Pittsburgh, disembarked at the house and stood drizzling and disconsolate, ringing on the knocker. There was no answer – and to Jackson, wet, impotent again and now bitterly frustrated with it, this was the Philadelphian *coup de grace* and the final straw. He would have to ferret about in his dissolving clothing for the ballast of formidable Hiscock Mincham Muschamp house-keys. He felt no tremor of gratitude that Kegan had "just in case" given them to him: "Anyone'd think they had the Hope Diamond!" he snarled, dankly searching and cursing; and there would be no pink and flustered Mercy to open the door. A garrison of locks defied him, and kept him on the step for a full fifteen minutes. Another fifteen minutes to get up to his room and undress, to avoid the reflection of his paunch in the mirror, to hide himself quickly in a robe, to go down and prepare a tray of tea and carry it up again to his bathroom. He sank into a scalding tub and began eating chocolate cookies. It was not as good as sex (nor as reducing), but it was balm to his soul.

* * *

For Mercy, also, this had not been a good day. She had waited ages for Grace so they could get on the Fairmount Park trolley, and when Grace had appeared at last on Kennedy Boulevard she had been wearing eye-black.

Then they had an especially peculiar trolley driver, who drove them fast round the places of interest and kept stopping beside the tennis courts and the sports fields.

Then Grace had insisted they get out and stroll around at the Japanese tea-house, and had only sat on a rock and waved at a swan because it became her so much.

Then the thunder-storm had started, and they'd had a very long wait for the next trolley, and they'd had to sit in their damp Clothes when it came, and when the ride ended it was just a little walk for Grace from the stop to the hotel, but for Mercy it was more than fourteen blocks.

It was a truly terrible way to have spent her free time, and that all of this should have happened on the Lord's Day!

Mercy splashed towards Society Hill through the downpour, and dwelt wretchedly on the long-lost pleasures of the Recreation Hour. The singing of Hopeful hymns around the piano, and the Eldresses reading aloud from the uplifting Phrasebook. The orderly, in-praise-of-the-Lord conversation, and the darning, and the making and mending of quilts. The drinking of milk and the eating of pie – several slices – and the talking about Titty, whether she was old enough to have her hems let down.

"Oooo, why did the Lord want me to be Hopeful in Philadelphia? I'm sure I could have been much more Hopeful if I'd stayed home!"

And Mercy's tears mingled with the rain, and ran down her cheeks and down inside her scratchy collar. (The lady had given her several sets of Clothes: three sets of good cloth and all the same for when she was indoors, working, and one of coarser stuff to wear for when she had her time off.)

It was terrible, too, to realise how very late she was now – how the waiting for the trolley in the storm had held her up. And perhaps Mr Jackson would be at the house already! She even had a pang of terror for a moment at the thought that Dr and Mrs Hiscock Mincham Muschamp might have cancelled their expedition for property, and be also there, waiting for her and cross.

She tried to hurry faster over the swimming sidewalks, and just as she was nearing their street she tripped and fell.

She landed on her palms and her knees, splash and crunch on the cobbles, and was in such pain that she could only limp along when she managed to get up.

For the first time since she had worked there, she actually wanted to be inside the blue front door. Weeping and limping, she only prayed that the house might be empty – that she might be able to make herself decent, before anyone saw.

She crawled up the steps, unfastened the door and then shut it behind her – and was met by Jackson, in a fresh shirt and trousers, and still very pink from his bath.

He was half-way into the drawing room, but he came straight back out again.

"Ah – you're wet through." To him, it sounded as though he'd said it optimistically.

"Y-yes, sir."

Jackson ventured up closer. "Did you know your knees are bleeding?"

"Y-y yes, s-sir." And Mercy sneezed.

"And you're getting a cold!"

"Ooooooo-"

"Have a handkerchief, here, and come with me." Jackson took her wet little hand in his and felt a distinct sensation, and led her up the stairs and into his room, and through it into his bathroom. His bathroom was still very warm, and smelled of soap-on-a-rope. There was also the tray with the dirty tea-things, and the smeared remains of chocolate. "I'm going to run you a bath." At fifty-seven, a man could be masterful.

"Oooooo – "

"Oh, yes, I am, child. I'm old enough to be your father." Jackson had the shame to turn away at this hypocrisy. "And you're going to get out of those wet clothes, and you're going to soak, and I'm going to go downstairs and make you tea."

"Ooooo, but –"

"The only tasteful thing in this house is the Earl Grey tea. I drank it and thanked God Cordelia's a snob. Now, that's the tub filling and I'll go and you can get out of those clothes."

"N-no." Mercy stood, biting her lips and dripping.

"For God's sake, child, I'm not going to be here to watch you."

The bluster covered a depth of great regret.

"N-no, sir. B-but –"

"What then?"

"B-but th-thee's got mirrors."

"*What*?"

"Thee's got mirrors in thy bathroom. I've taken all the mirrors out of mine."

"You've – Do you mean to tell me you won't undress where there's a mirror?"

"I d-don't th-think I sh-should, sir."

"Well." Jackson was nonplussed. "Can't you cover them up?"

"N-no, I c-can't, sir. Not when they're all over the walls, and all. C-couldn't I *p-please* go up to *my* room?"

Jackson turned off the taps. He pushed the plunger and opened the bath drain. One feeling awkward, panting, and the other feeling grateful, dripping, they threaded their way farther up through the house.

Jackson hesitated to get his breath at the door of Mercy's bedroom – it was so much smaller and more intimate and more pure than his own. He could not rush in and run water, nor pour essence in this bath for her. Mercy limped about, wiping her nose on his handkerchief; she was suddenly on her own ground and almost self-sufficient. "I can still make that tea," he suggested, gulping valiantly.

"Ooooo, no, sir! Please, sir, no, really –"

"It's no trouble." And he was plumply gone.

Jackson, recovered and making tea in the kitchen, tutted to himself when he wasn't singing. That child up there – eighteen with the mind of an eight-year-old. And direct from the last century. He found more cookies and filled a plate with them – a child like her would appreciate sweet things. He took pains with the tray, and with the tea-making – give her time to relax and soak in the tub. But still he found himself hurrying up the stairs only twelve minutes after he had come down.

It delayed him a while, though, panting on the landings.

He paused outside her bedroom door, eventually. Coughed, to

cover a gasp. Should he knock? He called "Mercy?" and heard a little shriek and a lot of splashing. "Don't worry, I'll let myself in, and I'll stay in the bedroom!" He carried the tray to the bed, set it down and sat down beside it, eyes drawn irresistibly to the magnet bathroom door. There were more splashings, and flip-flap wet-foot noises. When she appeared, it was in a strange construction of bath towels. "Don't you have a robe?" he croaked. The child quite obviously should be declared a protected species; she was so defenceless she shouldn't be let out alone. Perhaps, with the help of a strong father figure. . . .

"No, sir. Mrs Hiscock Mincham Muschamp didn't think I needed it."

Mrs Hiscock Mincham Muschamp had here also abandoned her thick shag-pile carpet. There were a few worn scatter rugs on the polished boards.

"Drink your tea."

"Yes, sir." Mercy sat down obediently, and began sipping, pink and warm damp. Her hair was wet, and Jackson rubbed it with a towel for her. Her feet were beaded with water, and he dried those. She ate a cookie, with a peaceful expression. She said, "Oooooo" and looked over her grazes and her feet at him, and said, "This is just like the Lord's Day I was thinking of."

"It is?"

"When it was raining, before I fell over. I was thinking of how it would be now, back in the settlement."

Jackson got off his knees again and sat on the bed with her. He used the towel to wipe his forehead. "Kegan said you were Amish."

"No, sir. I'm Hopeful."

"Ah."

"It would be the Recreation Hour now, with the Eldresses –" Mercy gave a little sob, wiped her nose on a towel-edge, bit into a cookie and went on. "We'd be singing and mending, and reading from the Phrasebook –"

"What Phrasebook?"

"The Phrasebook of Uplift. It has all the wisdom thee needs to guide thee through life."

"Good God. Is it published?"

"I beg thy pardon, sir?"

"Never mind. What else would thee – I mean, what else would you be doing?"

"Grace would be dancing. Grace just loves dancing. And Mother Germaine might be quilting, and there'd be conversation, and Wet Bottom Shoo Fly Pie."

Jackson considered her. "I can see how little Philadelphia has to offer you in exchange for all that."

"Oooooo, sir!" Mercy wept and choked on a cookie. "I'm just so miserable and I want to go home!"

"Well, great Heavens, child, why don't you?"

"Because I just can't – not without – no, I can't tell thee. Ooooo, sir, if thee only knew how terrible it is out in The World after our lovely settlement. Thee can't imagine how beautiful it is there, and green, and there aren't any noises, and no horseless carriages –"

"Good God, it's a wonder the place isn't over-run."

"Oooooo-oooooh!" And Mercy put her head on his shoulder, which was almost exactly what he'd wanted her to do. And he patted her hair, which curled obligingly round his fingers, and he took the cookie out of her mouth and kissed the chocolatey dribble, and he hugged her and rocked her backwards and forwards (this went on for some time). And he unwrapped some towelling and found a breast, and unwrapped more layers and kissed her all over. And became highly excited and undid his own things.

And discovered the biggest erection that he'd ever had.

So big in fact that it quite dwarfed his paunch.

Jackson was so overwhelmed by it that he wanted to keep an eye on it, and behaved with Mercy like a man watching his feet while dancing.

And Mercy cried "Ooooo!" a great deal, which was nothing to go by because she was always doing that, but there was a certain gurgle to the "Ooooo!" which hadn't been there before. And Jackson, who had never in his life had a virgin, experienced a momentary horror that he might hurt her, but was so worked up at the red-hot thought of deflowering an eighteen-year-old when he was fifty-seven, and when he hadn't been in a position to deflower a handkerchief for the past five years, that his reservations only occurred to him when he was already inside her, and then he could distinctly feel that it was far too late.

Mercy was so tight that in an ecstasy he smothered her and called her his Penis Fly Trap, and was amazed and rewarded by the amount of noise she made – like a cat having kittens – and the number of times during the aeon that followed when Mercy's having kittens went on.

To him, and rather late (though better late than never) had come a revelation: sex was like *this*.

Jackson had laboured hard and long over an unresponsive Sylvia, who had done nothing but give him bad reviews. Attacked below the belt, he had begun suffering from the limp spaghetti syndrome even before she issued the hat ultimatum and slammed expensively out of his life.

Now he could believe neither his luck nor his own virile condition – as far as he could judge, Mercy had had about fourteen orgasms, but beyond that the bed had floated away and he had lost count.

* * *

Mercy didn't know anything about orgasms; she just knew something Almighty had happened to her. And when she lay glistening with sweat, hugged up close to cuddly Jackson, and finally able to stop whimpering, "Ooooo! Thank thee, thank thee!", her first coherent notion was that the Lord had answered her prayers.

On His Own Day he had sent her the longed-for convert; she and dearest Jackson could go home to Intercourse.

"I love thee," she said, while Jackson was kissing her between the legs again, and being held about nine inches above the mattress by another glorious evidence of life eternal.

"Ummmm," mumbled Jackson. And he paused in what he was doing, and caressed himself, and with tears in his eyes and genuine piety said, "Jesus Christ, look at that."

XI

The Hiscock Mincham Muschamps did not return that night. They telephoned at half past ten, in an advanced state of paralysis, to tell Jackson that they had run into (literally – Cordelia had been driving) the Reilly Blandford Buckleys who had never liked that fender anyway.

The Reilly Blandford Buckleys had a place in Harvey Cedars, and they had invited Kegan and Cordelia back for the evening, and what with the storm and the fender and the Chevas Regal, and the place in Harvey Cedars being one of the very best properties in Long Beach Island, the Hiscock Mincham Muschamps were staying over now, until tomorrow. Kegan didn't have any appointments on Monday mornings (nobody seemed to want to be seen by their proctologist Monday mornings) so they wouldn't be getting back till around noon and they'd miss him, wouldn't they. They had sounded positive.

"No," said Jackson blithely. "I don't have to leave for a while yet. So that's just fine, isn't it?"

A hand had been placed over the 'phone in Long Beach Island. Inadequately. Cordelia had been heard to splutter, "*How* long?" and Jackson had relaxed in a warm glow of pride and murmured to himself, "If only you knew".

Kegan had come back abruptly into focus; his headache had been audible, down the 'phone. "That's great, Jackson. Hah – how long can you stay? Next weekend?" There had been a squawk in the background and the hand went over the mouthpiece again.

Moments passed. Then the line cleared for the heavy breathing. "This Wednesday?"

"It's all still very vague, Kegan. Let's talk about it when you get back."

"Hah –"

"Goodnight, Kegan. Give my regards to Cordelia." Jackson hung up the kitchen 'phone. He was pleased to find that the milk had not boiled over (Mercy had wanted hot milk) and opened and shut cupboard doors, inquisitively. Rummaged in the refrigerator. Toasted things (he had a passion for toast buttered on both sides). Hummed to himself. Sang – a more robust song this time. A lyric of supreme obscenity, dealing with the improbable uses to which mature sailors could put their physical equipment. And mounted the stairs again.

"Mounted!" he puffed. And beamed, breathlessly. Everything had a new, happily lewd, connotation. Even the positions of the switches on the stove had been suggestive. The words on packages – *juicy, relish, succulent, full-bodied, wholesome* – had been relevant to a degree. The kitchen was a teaser's paradise. He virtually bolted the last flight ("Never felt fitter!" he triumphed) and collapsed in at the door of Mercy's room.

Mercy gleamed with a solid, holy radiance, like an illuminated chapter from the Bible; she pulsated good and golden love and actually lit up in the dark. Jackson stood at the foot of her bed, heaving. That something like this should happen to him. . . . That this lubricated angel should open a door in his life and raise him from the dead.

Mercy gazed adoringly at him. Jackson gazed adoringly at Mercy. Something incredible was happening to him below the waist.

For this he would have spent the rest of his days in a Society Hill attic, but it might not be necessary. . . . To take her back to the old, empty Colonial house and have her in every room in it. . . . The tray shook in his grasp. "Mercy," he panted, "what do you know about Pleasant Valley?"

* * *

Grace picked up the sheet, and shook it reproachfully. She said, "I only made up this room a few hours ago!"

The thin young man on the bed didn't answer. He was goggling at her as though he hadn't ever seen anyone naked.

"Does thou do this to thy bed at home?"

Still the young man didn't answer. He was holding on tightly to a book of the hotel matches. Then he swallowed, and lit a cigarette, and coughed his heart up. "Do you model?" he rasped, through the trembling smoke.

Grace giggled, and gathered more of the sheet from under a table. She knew he was staring as the fullnesses and hollows of her body moved. All the men asked did she model. The only difference was the time they asked, and the accent. She threw the bundle of sheet at the bed, playfully, and it landed in a crumpled, deflating balloon and slithered off his legs and on to the floor. The bedclothes had been dragged out and lay everywhere, and she skipped across the coverlet to the bathroom. Did she model!

Grace giggled again and pulled a face at herself in the mirror. "Thou liked me?" she shouted, and the man called, hoarsely, yes. She washed, her hair tied up out of the way with one of his ties; she cleaned her teeth, dried herself, and splashed herself all over with his cologne. She liked this man's cologne. It smelled of hayfields. Some of the men used cologne that smelled of rotting fruit.

She went back into the bedroom, found her scattered clothes, dressed, went to the bed and kissed him. She liked doing that, although his mouth was full of smoke and he coughed nervously. She liked kissing, if they would only let her, but they didn't all let her kiss them as long as she wanted, or if they did they were particular what she kissed.

She said goodnight to him, and smiled at him, and let herself out of the room and walked along the corridor to the elevator.

Four floors up, she got out of the elevator again and walked along that corridor to a door, and knocked. A man came to the door and let her in. He put his arms round her and his mouth on hers and slid his hand down over her behind so that he pressed his crotch hard against her. The light wasn't on and she couldn't remember what he looked like.

* * *

"But I can't go with thee!" wailed Mercy. "Thee knows, dearest, I told thee!"

Jackson struck the bedpost with his fist, screamed, examined his knuckles, and then said grumpily, "Why not?"

"It's to do with the Society, dearest."

Jackson reached the glass from the bedside cabinet and actually took a slug of the milk (now cold). He attempted to control himself. "I *know* it's to do with the Society, but if you don't tell me *what* it's to do with the Society, I'll turn you over and . . . I'll turn you over and – and –" He gripped the glass. "I'll paddle your – Oh, Christ."

"Are thee all right, dearest?"

Jackson took another swallow of the milk; it did nothing to calm him down. "I may have a coronary right here, the way things are going." He studied the pyramid he had created amidst the blankets and shook his fist at it. "Where were you when I needed you!"

"Dearest?"

"Not you, Mercy." More milk. "*Why* can't you come home with me?"

"Be-because thee's supposed to come home with *me*! Ooooooo!"

"What's the matter?"

"I never should have done it, I thought thee was sent by the Lord!"

"Oh my Christ."

"And now thee wants me to go with thee and Mother Germaine will be so cross!"

Jackson watched philosophically as the pyramid slowly subsided.

"I was only supposed to go as far as Philadelphia!"

"Well, you went a Hell of a lot farther than that tonight."

* * *

Grace edged her way up in the bed, heels, behind, elbows, and slowly, slowly, slipped her legs over the edge, her feet down on to the carpet, sat up, stood up, and stole away through the dimness.

He had turned his back and fallen immediately asleep and it would be a shame to wake him. A nice man, slow, not talkative, with hairs on his chest that had tickled her.

She shut the bathroom door before she turned the light on, and saw that her white breasts had been made pink by his tickling hair. The cool water soothed the pinkness, and she dabbed at it with the stuff from his bottle of mouth-wash: "Eases pain – fights infection".

Reflected in every wall by the mirrors, she turned and twisted, stretched and arched; and yawned, happily. As she moved about the bathroom, her reflection reminded her of something she had seen on a television engine, left on by a man just lately, in one of the bedrooms. It had been a sports programme.

She looked at herself and began to grin, and snatched up a towel to stifle a gurgle. She looked exactly like one of those people they called athletes, when the man had said they were limbering up.

* * *

"So thee sees thee has to come back with me, thee *has* to!" Mercy clutched at a pillow in an excess of anguish. "Oooooo, Jackson dearest, thee has to, else I have to go on looking for another convert –"

"I'll be damned if you do!"

"Ooooooo, dearest, please don't say such things, it's wicked!"

Jackson bit his glass-rim savagely. The thought of rapturously rosy Mercy trundling her adorable ass down the Eastern Seaboard, searching for converts for the Hopefuls, was enough to make him grind the glass and swallow it. "You're not going looking for anyone else!" he shouted at her.

"Ooooooo –"

"Oh, God." There was something about Mercy on the verge of tears that dragged Jackson and his coupling links towards her as inexorably as a magnet. All he could do was to flail helplessly in the wake of what felt like an Apollo mission aiming to dock. "You are not going looking for somebody else!" he threatened, rhythmically.

"Ooooooo-ooooo, Jackson."

"You are *not*, do you hear?"

"Ooooooo-ooooo." And Mercy, the sweetest cushion upon which any man might ever hope to lie, began having kittens again.

* * *

"You're kidding!"

"No!" Grace giggled.

"Caps and aprons and thee and thou and all that stuff?"

"Yes."

"Well –" The man laughed. He had dark hair, and a neat, trimmed moustache and beard, and a gold chain round his neck. Grace touched the chain. "Want it, honey?'

She bridled. Not much, but a little.

"Here." He took the chain off and fastened it round her neck. "Pretty titties you've got. So you came out from under all of that?"

She shook her head.

"You mean you still believe in it?"

She shook her head.

"C'mon, you don't want to talk, do you?"

She shook her head.

And he turned her over on to her stomach, and his mouth moist against her ear he said, "And now, kid, we are going to play choo-choo trains."

* * *

Some while later, when Jackson was getting in more supplies of hot milk and beigels, he lent his mind to the problem – as much because it vexed him as because he needed a distraction from the fact that everything below his neck ached.

There was absolutely no doubt that that eighteen-year-old child in the attic was the best thing that had ever happened to him. She was also likely to be the last thing that would happen to him, but what the Hell.

There was also no doubt that given the choice between his cosy old study in Upper New York State and what sounded like a Pennsylvania lunatic asylum for females, there was no choice at all. They'd probably only let him have Mercy once a year, anyway. Christmas. Or possibly Thanksgiving.

This time he carried the tray upstairs with greater caution. His age was beginning to tell. And, Jesus Christ, he was walking bow-legged.

He entered Mercy's little room masterfully. "Mercy," he choked (she was kneeling on the bed reading the Phrasebook: a picture for which Bob Guccione or Hugh Hefner would have mortgaged their empires, slavering), "Mercy, we have got to sort this out."

Mercy laid aside the Phrasebook. She had been puzzling over Phrase One hundred and ninety-six – "*Put thy hand on that which is important to thee and it will profit thee in The World*" – and wasn't quite sure at this moment what she should put her hand on.

"How the Hell could I help the Society, just by joining it?" Jackson sat down beside her, the tray across his knees. Mercy looked at him limpidly, the tray began to tilt, and Jackson groaned in agony. "Can't you put some clothes on," he pleaded weakly.

"Of course, dearest."

"The Hopefuls need converts you say, right?"

"Yes, dearest." Mercy was pulling on her nightdress, a voluminous calico effect brought into The World from the Settlement, which unfortunately for Jackson made her appear even more childishly nubile than she was.

"Because you don't have any men left, right?"

"Y-yes, dearest."

"But it's ridiculous. How could I possibly help them? You want a farmer, or a cow herd, some kind of handyman – or a builder – and I'm not religious, I wouldn't know how to ring a bell for services!"

"No, no, dearest, thee doesn't – I can't –" Mercy finished buttoning herself up to the neck, accepted a glass off the tray and sipped at it, colouring markedly. It was altogether one thing to *do* what she had done; it was another to talk about it, to a gentleman, out loud. "We don't have any Elders left in the Society," she began, "not since poor dear Brother Orville –"

"Yes, yes, you said all that."

"And if we don't get any, the Hopefuls will all just die out."

"You mean there'll be no-one to do the hard work and the farming around the place."

"No, dearest, Hopeful women have always done most of that. Hopeful men think on higher things."

Jackson stared at Mercy. If all the Hopeful women looked like her, he could just imagine what higher things the Hopeful men were thinking on. Not to mention why they were too tired to do any hard work.

"Oh, please, dearest, it's so difficult. . . . And thee's so clever, doesn't thee understand? If there aren't any men in the Society –" Mercy faltered, and went completely crimson, as far as the eye could see. "There won't be any new Hopeful babies, will there?"

Jackson gaped. Stupefied. "Babies? *Babies*?" He got up, put the tray down, paced about the room, stopped short – "*Babies*! You mean you want a *stud*, Mercy, not a convert!"

"Ooooooo –"

"Now don't you start that again, I'll have an anxiety attack! Babies." Jackson shook his head hopelessly. "Well, that's that, you can't take me home."

"But I can, I can! Ooooooo, please, dearest –"

"I'd be no use to you."

"Yes, thee would!"

"No, I wouldn't."

"Oooooooo, please –"

"No."

"Why *not*, dearest?"

"After the divorce –" He scratched his neck. Sniffed.

"Yes?"

"After the divorce, I thought what the Hell, things can only get better, I –"

"Yes, dearest?"

"I had a vasectomy."

* * *

At three o'clock in the morning, in room 6004, Grace finally came. It was the sixth room she'd been in that night, of course – the usual. Not that she went in six rooms every night, but that when she *did* go in the rooms it wasn't until the fifth or the sixth that she had something more than just fun happen to her. The first few times she'd imagined it was to do with the man, or the technique, so she'd go to the sixth room first the next night, but that didn't work, it made no difference. She just enjoyed herself in four or five rooms, and the men she was enjoying herself with worked above and beneath her like engines, and glorious ripples and waves ran up and down her body and she giggled and wriggled and whispered into their ears the outlandish things they liked to hear, and dressed up if they wanted her to, or was naked if they wanted that; and then by the time the sixth door had closed behind her she was loose, tight, at a pitch, languid, ready, and whoever she was with, an old man or a young man, a clever lover or a clumsy one, she died and cried and drowned with him in the warm, stale air of the sixth bedroom.

It had been like that from the beginning. At least, from the time she had got as far as six bedrooms. And even before that, she had always loved what she was doing – what she had wanted to be doing for so very long. She had set off on it ravenously, her *à la carte* journey, and consultations with Beatrice in the YWCA kitchen had ensured she took precautions against putting on a lot of weight. Even at the beginning she had made very few mistakes. And those she had made had turned out to be all for the good in the long run. She had lowered her lashes to a mild-appearing man, for her first lover: pale face, pale suit, spectacles, slope-shouldered – Hopefully, *surely* small. Bearing in mind her virginity. But he'd turned out to have the biggest cock in America. This had meant being hurt much more than she'd wanted, but for a much shorter time. It had also meant that she only got as far as room number four that night, being still tender, and was stuck at the enjoyment stage for a week before she worked up to six bedrooms.

The night she hit the sixth bedroom had been a night to remember. The man in it was a foreigner – a Swede she thought he'd said – who had picked her up in his arms and carried her around the room before he laid her on the bed. Mostly, they were not that energetic. Mostly, they were somehow transfixed by her – until they in their turn transfixed her, against walls or in showers or on rumpled sheets she had smoothed the same morning.

The Swede had held her against him, and had told her there was a saying in a foreign language, something like "a voice calls to me in the woods and I answer it", and he told her that that was what it was like, making love to her.

She had rushed to his room the following evening, but nothing had happened there except the enjoyment, and in the sixth room that night she found a short, balding man from Detroit.

* * *

"I tell you, you are not going round hooking some other convert!" Jackson was sore in delicate places, and beside himself. "I don't care a damn about your confounded Society!"

"Oooooo –"

"I want you, and I *don't* want you laying eggs all over Pennsylvania just to keep the fucking Hopefuls up to scratch!"

"*Oooooo* –"

"Oh, *Christ*." And Jackson threw himself down in a chair, and leapt up again. Cane-bottom chairs are not good for large bare behinds. "Somebody else can go round drumming up converts!"

"Somebody else *is*, Jackson dearest, I *told* thee."

"No, you didn't!"

"Yes, dearest, I promise thee, dearest, I did too. I told thee when –" Her lips trembled. "I told thee I came here with Grace."

"Oh, God, and I thought you were talking holy. Is this Grace a person?"

"Yes, Jackson dearest."

"What's she look like?"

Mercy frowned for a moment.

"I mean, is she pretty?"

Mercy still looked troubled. Then she said, "Thee knows that big painting of the lady outside the motion picture house on Chestnut Street?"

"Where they're showing the Jane Russell retrospective? Don't tell me –"

"Well, part of Grace looks like that."

Jackson sank down on the bed. "Which part?" Mercy blushed and made a gesture. "Jesus Christ."

"And thee knows the store window with all the journals on Walnut Street?"

"The one that sells continental magazines? They've got a display of – Oh my God, not Claudia Cardinale."

"Well, Grace does have red hair but the rest of her looks like that."

Jackson sat staring into space. He was wondering whether he could conceivably have got the wrong end of the lollipop. Then he considered the way he was feeling and had to acknowledge that if he'd got the right end of the lollipop he would quite probably have been dead by now.

Mercy was looking at him worriedly. She said, "Grace is working in a terrible place."

"What's that?"

"It's a hotel. It's over by Thirtieth Street Station."

"What does she do?"

"She does what I do."

"God help them."

"Pardon, dearest?"

"I'm sorry."

"I meant she's a maid."

Jackson would have smoked a cigar, if he smoked. "Let me get this absolutely clear. You left this place in the back of beyond Lancaster, and you were supposed to get converts for the Society so that you could have football teams of kids and the Hopefuls would populate the earth."

Mercy wrung her hands. "Ooooo, Jackson, thee makes it sound so terrible!"

"I got it right then. And this other girl, Grace, the one with the red hair and the – She's supposed to be finding these converts too?"

"Y-yes, dearest."

"Then why don't we leave it to her?"

Mercy twisted a bit of calico nightdress between her fingers. "Jackson, I think Grace has lost her faith."

Jackson tore at his grey hair. "What the Hell does *that* mean?"

"She's started wearing lip-rouge, and to-day she had on eye-black!"

"Thank Christ for that. I was beginning to be afraid she might be hiding her light under a bushel."

"I wish thee wouldn't speak that way, Jackson dearest." Mercy moped into her calico. "It sounds so Worldly."

"Mercy, one of us has got to be worldly around here! Let's face it, she's going to get a whole lot more converts if she makes the most of her natural advantages. And she's probably just going through some kind of crisis of faith, coming in contact with the outside world and all that. She'll play around –" Jackson bit back his words, seeing by Mercy's terrified expression that he might be going rather too far. "But she'll find the right person! And then all she'll want to do is go right back home to your Society and settle down and raise a family and be a good little Hopeful." May God forgive me, he prayed, for deceiving this innocent, concupiscent little baby.

The concupiscent little baby was still twisting her nightdress. "Does thee really think so, Jackson dearest?"

"Yes, I really think so. And I devoutly hope so. Because you don't want to go haring off all over the country looking for converts, do you?"

"Oooooo, nooooo!" And Mercy burst into tears.

"Do you think you'll find anyone suitable here with Cordelia and Kegan? Anyone apart from me, that is?"

"Noooo!"

"Don't you want to get away from the city and into the country?"

"Y-yes, Jackson dearest. Ooooo, y-yes."

"So that's all right then. Now, is there anything else worrying you?" He patted Mercy's cuff. "Were you supposed to bring back a convert each?"

Mercy wept copiously into her nightdress. Finally she managed, "I-I th-think s-so."

"O.K. Grace'll have to find two."

"Jackson!" Baby was so horrified she sucked her tears back in her eyes. "That's *sinful*!"

"She needn't have them both for herself, she could bring back a spare one. He could help around the Settlement till the babies start growing up, and then he could marry off with one of them. You hear about it in Tennessee all the time."

Mercy snuffled. "D-d-d-does th-thee *really* th-think so?"

"Absolutely." Jackson signed exhaustedly, and cuddled Mercy to him. "There you are, everything's taken care of. You can come home with me to Pleasant Valley, I'll look after you, you'll look after me and we'll both drink a lot of milk."

She gazed up at him, still somewhat doubtful.

"I'll teach you how to type my manuscripts, it'll be wonderful."

"B-but –"

"After all, you couldn't go back without a convert, could you?"

"N-no –"

"They wouldn't be very pleased with you, would they?"

"Noooooo – "

"And would you really want to take anyone else but me?"

"Oooooo! Ooooooo, no, Jackson, I love thee!"

"Then you'll just have to come and he hopeful in Pleasant Valley." Jackson patted her again, and cuddled her, and felt a quite unmistakeable stirring, as though a sleeping animal had risen on its forepaws and was sniffing the air. "And – oh God – you two girls can have a little talk and – oh Christ – we'll leave it all to Grace and – oh –"

"Ooooooo-oooooooo!"

XII

The trolley rattled across the huge bridge, enclosed by the peeling young leaf colour of the painted ornamental ironwork. "Where *is* Pleasant Valley?" asked Grace.

"It's hours away from here, just hours." Mercy's misery conjured up vast, immeasurable distances. "It's farther north than New York."

The trolley went on rattling. Grace said, "Isn't that Canada?"

"No." The blonde snuffled and mopped. "It's in New York State."

The girls were doing what they always did when they wanted to talk: they were riding around on the Fairmount Park Trolley. By now they knew as much about the ride as the driver, and could have recited by rote the commentary: Fairmount Park was the largest park in the world (it was even the largest park in Pennsylvania); it covered eight thousand acres (and some of it was good grazing land); it had elegant authentic Colonial mansions, where you could get out and walk and see the elegance (and the authentics); it had a zoological gardens (and one of the creatures was a Safari Monorail); it had summertime entertainment: Robin Hood Dell West, where there was serious music and an orchestra; the Playhouse in the Park, where there were dramatics – and sometimes plays; and Robin Hood Dell East, where there was unserious music and things called ethnics.

It was a very fine day today, and the green and red trolley with its yellow window-edging had bowled through the traffic, along the Parkway, past the Rodin Museum (the largest collection of Rodins outside France – Grace had suggested Rodins might be some kind of dessert), past the golden statue of the lady riding astride with a long pole in her hand (Joan of Arc, she was named by the commentary), and across the parklands.

The girls rocked and slithered and bounced on the slatted seats.

"I think thou's very lucky," said Grace, above the rattle. "There it was in the Phrasebook – *'No field is too large for the Hopeful plough'.*" And she fondled the chain about her neck, with a reminiscent smile.

"But I don't want to go!"

An elderly couple across the aisle with a camera apparatus stared and then bent towards each other, to whisper.

"I don't want to go anywhere except the Society, I just want to go home to the Settlement!" Mercy waved her handkerchief at the strange mushroom structure of the Playhouse in the Park (Dracula was showing). "Jackson won't come with me, he just won't, and I don't know what to do."

"Thou's a very ungrateful girl, and thou knows exactly what thou should do." The chain slid between Grace's fondling fingers. "Thou's found a man thou loves, and he loves thee, and he's taking thee back home with him to this Pleasant Valley. I wish I could see what thy trouble is, Mercy, but I truly can't."

"But I don't want to go! I want to go back home to –"

"Oh, shut thy mouth." Grace fidgeted, irritated. "I don't think thee can remember the Settlement properly, thou's so stupid over it. Milking and hoeing and scrubbing and starching, and no mirrors. And no men. No men, Mercy. Has thou really forgotten what it was like, having to take a bath in cold water?"

"Unless I'm sick, I still do!"

"Thou's not going to tell me thou's forgotten the underwear? Those long, scratchy –"

Mercy blushed deeply. That morning Jackson had smuggled her his very first present: five sets of tiny, lace-trimmed silk drawers.

"And here's a man come along who wants to take thee away from being a maid to those Mincham Muschamps, and off to his home with him –"

"Yes, Jackson does say it's pretty." The blonde head bent lower over the crumpled handkerchief. "He says he has a lot of ground, and if I wanted I could have hens and sheep."

The trolley shuddered past a white stone statue of Moses pointing towards Heaven.

"Well then."

"But, Grace," the whimpering voice sank lower and lower, along with the head. "Grace, I don't like The World."

The elderly couple were standing in the back of the trolley, snapping away with their apparatus. Grace wasn't sure quite what to do with Mercy. She *never* knew quite what to do with Mercy. Being with Mercy was like being with a premature baby.

"Grace, thee knows right from the start how I've hated The World. It's not peaceful, Grace, and it's not Godly, and there's no time to spend sitting around just being good and eating –"

"Shoo Fly Pie!" Her companion made retching noises. "It was so *fattening*!"

"Thee never used to talk that way, thee never used to say things were *fattening*. And thee never wore lip-rouge nor eye-black neither, and thee never smelled of stuff too."

The redhead, for the first time, looked alarmed. "What do I smell of?"

"Thee smells of that French stuff – like Mrs Hiscock Mincham Muschamp's dressing table."

"Oh well." Grace fanned herself relievedly with an open hand.

"It's all wrong, Grace, it's not right and it's not Godly and it's not Hopeful and I don't like it." Mercy's head was bent so low she was showing a shocking amount of the nape of her neck. "Things were all straight in the Settlement. There was wrong and there was right and if it was wrong thee didn't do it." A sniff. "Out in The World thee could spend thy whole life searching and waiting around for something right to do. Why, I can't even make out some of the Phrasebook of Uplift any more! The only thing I'm sure of out in The World now is Jackson's a good man – I know he is and I want to save his soul."

The redhead's open hand closed, and clenched on her neck chain.

"I want to save his soul, Grace, I want him to become a Hopeful."

Grace addressed the top of her head: "Has thou told him?"

"No, I was going –"

"I wouldn't. Not yet, if I were thee. But why doesn't thou go and save his soul in Pleasant Valley?"

"There isn't a Hopeful Settlement in Pleasant Valley! There'd be no other Sisters!" Mercy uttered a whine. "I wouldn't know who to ask about what was unGodly – I might let poor Jackson be ensnared by the work of the Devil – I might get confused about the Phrases. . . . There was always Mother Germaine or Sister Agatha, or Sister Unity or Sister Amy – they always knew what we should do. They used to tell us, and it was orderly, and it was simple and I don't like mirrors. And I never minded the cold water!"

"Well, thou would have a man now, I suppose, and he'd keep thee warm."

The trolley swung along the parkways, the commentary flickered on and off and the elderly couple went on whispering and snapping. Grace began to feel a certain relenting towards the prostrated Mercy. The whimpering little blonde looked so pathetic. So wistful. What a problem it must be, being so good.

"Thou says he lives in the country?"

The prostrate blonde raised her crumpled face and her brimming eyes.

"Thy nose is running."

"Ooo, I'm sorry, Grace." She rubbed around with her handkerchief. "Yes, he lives in the country."

"Well, if he likes the country anyway, perhaps he might get to like the Society. If thou made sure to show it to him in warm weather. . . . And when Sister Heloise was upstairs. . . . If thou could get him back to the Settlement with thee for a visit, perhaps he might stay and then that would make everything all right."

"Yes, but he won't come." Mercy sobbed. "He can't have babies."

Grace took her shoulder and shook it. "Mercy, we've all been telling thee since thou was thirteen years old – *girls* are the ones who have the babies!"

"Yes, I know, I do know now, Grace, but he can't – he –" Mercy drizzled. "He explained to me, but I didn't understand it all. He just keeps saying if the Society needs men because of new babies, he isn't Hopeful."

The trolley ground between the Memorial Arches.

Grace frowned. "I don't remember Mother Germaine saying anything about us making conditions for converts like that."

Mercy mourned at her, lips parted, dripping, as though the Phrasebook itself were being poured out of Grace line by line. As indeed it was, so very often, despite the fact that Grace had become so disturbingly Worldly.

"Mother Germaine told us we were to go out into The World in search of converts for the Hopefuls. I know she explained the Society would die out without men, Mercy, but she was so itty-bitty about it she never actually said they all had to be able to breed children." The slender fingers fondled the chain again. "And anyway, how were we supposed to know? How were we supposed to find out if they could be fathers? We were supposed to keep our aprons down and our drawers up and keep a hold on our Phrasebook."

"Oooo, Grace!"

"What were we supposed to do? Go up to men and say, 'Please come and be a Hopeful, what's thy sperm count?'"

"What's a –"

"Never mind." Grace shrugged her lovely bosom, expertly. "If thou finds a man and takes him home with thee, that ought to be enough for anybody." She considered the wet Hopeful. "I'll bet it's more than they expected."

"*Yes*, Grace, but Jackson won't go!" Mercy drummed on the wooden seat wretchedly. "I keep telling thee. I do love him so much, and I said maybe God would give us babies anyway, even if he has had a voluptuary. But then he said he couldn't face the Settlement, with it just being a lot of women. He likes mixed company, Grace, and he says he'd miss the telephone. And he belongs to some kind of *circle*, the same as Dr Hiscock Mincham Muschamp, and they all read stories about an Englishman in a funny hat. Jackson showed me his picture in a book, Grace, and he had a pipe, just like poor dear Brother Orville. Jackson gets a lot of mail about all that and he has to use the telephone, and he goes to

New York City too, because he writes books –" Mercy ran out of breath. "I don't think he'd mind the Society so much if they had a telephone and it wasn't all women."

Grace sat and stared at the back of the trolley driver's neck. "Oh well," she said. And that was all she said for a very long while.

* * *

The trolley was rounding a street perimeter of the park on its homeward journey. It passed houses with glassed-in porches, the glass smashed and the walls covered in daubs. "Park Manor," Grace read to herself, as she always did, "four thousand Parkside Apartments" and gazed at the broken-windowed, desolate, sleazy building. A policeman sat on some steps along the sidewalk, eating a sandwich. He didn't move to look at the trolley. All of the other people along the sidewalk looked at the trolley. All of the other people along the sidewalk were black.

The blonde snuffled miserably at her end of the seat. "It's all right for thee."

Grace turned to blink at her. "What's that thou said?"

Mercy wriggled. "I didn't mean anything bad, I just said it was all right for thee. Thee's so – thee's so – thee could find a convert. Thee can go back whenever thee wants."

"But I won't, because I don't want."

The two girls faced one-another, Grace calmly, Mercy damp, in horror. "Thee can't mean it, Grace, thee just can't mean it. Jackson said –" She swallowed, and gulped to a stop.

"What?" A flush began seeping up from the redhead's gleaming bosom. "*What* did Jackson say?"

"Jackson s-said th-thee'd go back to the Society with a convert for thyself and a convert for me, too, and that would s-settle – that would s-solve everything."

"Oh well. Oh. Well. Did he? Well I'm not going back to the Settlement *ever*. Never, ever, ever. Never. So there." And Grace got out a mirror and a little box and slapped green powder all over her eyelids.

Mercy would have thrown herself through the trolley window at this dreadful moment, if it hadn't been for the grille.

The ride continued. The commentary told them what they already knew, that the azalea garden behind Boat House Row contained two thousand azaleas. Several Japanese people got on, and the elderly couple got off the trolley. When it came to its last stop before returning to John F. Kennedy Boulevard, Grace suddenly stood and dragged Mercy up with her. "We're getting out," she said.

"But th-this is the Art Museum!"

"Don't worry, I'm not taking thee in to see nude pictures, we haven't finished talking yet!"

They clambered down off the trolley and Grace stomped over to sit on the steps in the sunshine. "Thou wants to go back to the Society," she began stormily.

Mercy crouched feebly beside her. "Yes, I –"

"And I don't. And thou loves Jackson, and he loves thee, but he won't settle in the Society with it just being all women. No, keep thy mouth shut – don't say anything, I'm thinking." Grace twiddled with a lock of her glorious red hair. The passing men stopped passing. One got out his apparatus and took a photograph. "I have to tell thee, Mercy, and thou's got to understand, I'm not going back there – not with only a man or two. It'd have to be six of them. It'd have to be six at least. And they'd have to have a room each. It'd mean there'd be more company for Jackson, but I can't see it happening. Can thou see it happening? And even if I could get the six of them back to the Settlement, I wouldn't want to stay there myself. Hoeing and milking and starching –"

Mercy gaped at her.

"Jackson thinks I'm like thee, does he? That's how he got this idea? he thinks I'd want to go back, and I'm Godly and Hopeful, and I don't like The World, and I miss the cold baths?"

The blonde bundle looked shifty.

"Or has thou been telling him things? Thou has, has thou. Mercy, thou bitch."

"Oooo, Grace –"

"Thou hasn't changed, thou's been a sneak always. And he's no better than thee – selling me down the river to the Settlement just because –"

"Please, Grace! Please, please, don't be angry!"

Grace had flaming red patches in her creamy pale cheeks. "Well, I'm not going back there. No, I'm not, ever. I *like* The World. And I'm not leaving it to be holy and get chapped hands, and eat fattening old Wet Bottom Shoo Fly Pie."

They sat, flaming righteousness and craven cowardice, on the stone steps. A Japanese sight-seer took sixteen reels of them.

Mercy exhausted her handkerchief and all her hems.

The sun sank lower, and the towers and blocks of the city grew misty in the soft haze, and the stone steps became harder, and the Art Museum reared vast and shadowy behind them, and Grace grew tired of being cross.

She had been too used, for too long, to looking after and forgiving Mercy. It was altogether too much of an effort to try and change the habit now.

More time passed. Her cheeks had cooled down. She said grudgingly, "I'm still trying to think of something."

There was a wail from beneath a green horse statue. "So's Jackson! He's still trying to think of something, too."

"Jackson's already thought of something, hasn't he?" Grace lifted her chin. "And I'm it!"

"No! Oo, no, he's still thinking and thinking, because I told him what a temple of the Devil it is, that place where thee's working. Every night I've been telling him – how terrible it is, and how unGodly – and he's started to worry thee might not be able to find a convert there after all."

The redhead edged closer. "How many nights has thou been telling him?"

"Ever since Sunday."

Grace pursed her lips approvingly. "Thou has been a busy little Hopeful."

They looked at each-other, and the dusky heat of the city, the scent of the dust, and the blossoms, and the leaves, and the gasoline, rose around them. Mercy sniffed. "Jackson was wondering. . ."

"Yes?"

"Jackson was wondering whether thee c-could c-convert a

friend of his."

There was no answer.

Mercy gathered her hems, and her confidence. "H-he's got this f-friend, Grace, this friend in Washington, and h-he's a bachelor, and J-Jackson keeps saying he needs a housekeeper, and h-he's a poor wifeless soul, a-and J-Jackson th-thought if th-thee could go and keep h-house for him. . . . If thee d-doesn't have any l-luck at the h-hotel."

"Oh yes."

"A-and if th-thee couldn't convert him, perhaps thee c-could c-convert one of his friends? Or t-two? Or th-three of them?"

"Two or three . . . Has he got many friends?"

"H-he must have. Jackson says he knows a lot of people. He works in –" Mercy hesitated, and mouthed the word with difficulty. "The P-Pentagon?"

Grace smoothed her blouse, and Mercy glanced away hurriedly (she could see through it). And Grace wasn't wearing her camisole.

"Thou knows I'm not going back to the Settlement! But it might be nice to *see* Washington. . . ." she said. "One of my – one of the hotel guests gave me his card and he comes from there." She was trying to remember which of the guests it had been. She had a feeling that it was a sixth roomer. But whether it was a Swede, or an Englishman, or a Virginian. . .

"If thee w-went down to Washington, if Jackson thought thee was w-working –" The blonde bit her lips. "I could keep on telling him, reading to him from the Phrasebook, showing him the Hopeful ways. . . . Perhaps he'd come to see the light, if I was to reveal the teachings to him after supper. Perhaps he'd let us have a Recreation Hour." She concentrated, wrinkling her pink and white brow at the stone steps in front of her. "If I had enough time, I might bring him round – bring him back to see the Settlement on a visit – just so long as he thinks thee's the one finding the converts, not me."

The redhead drew away and stared in admiration. "Mercy! And I never thought thou had a crust of brain in thy head."

"It mustn't take me too long though, to save him. It'd be just terrible if he died unHopeful, and I hadn't saved his soul."

Grace's green eyelids widened. "Is he likely to die, then?"

"He keeps saying so. Every night he tells me that, Grace, and then he says what a way to go."

"Oh well –" And Grace, to the delight of the late-afternoon watchers, began giggling and laughing and gurgling till she rolled about temptingly in the shadow of the hallowed portals of the Philadelphia Museum of Art.

XIII

The Hiscock Mincham Muschamps did not take it well. In fact they took it very ill indeed. Not that Mercy was leaving them (which they did not know about), nor that she was leaving them for Jackson (about which they knew even less), nor that she and Jackson were currently breaking the all-comers record in their attic (which, being buffered by malt liquors, they did not even suspect). But that Jackson was still staying with them after ten days.

They began, roughly speaking, to treat him as an old fixture. Cordelia went to her Committees, and stalled her Mercedes, and lay down with her heads. Kegan went to his office and, as late as possible, came home again. And they attended dinner parties to which they always ostentaciously invited Jackson, hoping they could sick him off on to some other couple, and Jackson always thanked them and said he'd prefer to stay home and get in an early night. There would be icy good-byes and the slamming of doors in the airy evenings.

Jackson would then rush round for provender and take it up to the attic and Mercy, and when they were not doing noisy, sticky, surprisingly splendid and exciting things to one-another, or having a rest and reconsidering doing it, Jackson was persuading Mercy of the glorious future they would have in Pleasant Valley, where there was a double bed and she could learn how to be his typist, and Mercy was telling Jackson how good it was being a Hopeful, and what a considerable while one's soul spent in Eternity after one was dead, and they were both engaged in the removal of their Great Hope Grace to Washington.

This took time, and skill, and many costly long distance telephone calls to Washington (costly to the Hiscock Mincham Muschamps). For Jackson's friend was first away, and then busy, and then alarmed, suspicious, reluctant and finally *coy* at the prospect of acquiring a housekeeper.

Jackson put down the receiver after one of these conversations and swore for ten minutes. "It's not as if he's *happy* the way he is!" he fumed penultimately. "Living alone with a Diners Card in Foggy Bottom –"

Mercy peered over a muffin. "I thought thee said he lived in Washington."

"He lives in a section of Washington that's called Foggy Bottom. It's – well –" Jackson forced his hands through his hair; he felt baffled and thwarted. "It's quaint, and it has a lot of trees and shrubbery. And little dogs, and Siamese cats on leashes. It's full of secretaries who work on the Hill, and young GS9s." Mercy opened her mouth again. "Government Servants. They're graded by numbers, and 9s aren't very much of anything. Twatchel's so senior to them he can't mix with them socially. He only sees them in the Watergate, buying pastries."

The manoeuvre was taking far more coercion on Jackson's part than he had imagined, and he began to wonder whether some other permanent house-guest was having to be ousted by his Washington fellow-Sherlockian and member of The Red Circle scion society there, Twatchel Clootie. Certainly Twatchel might be said to be havering; Jackson had the uncomfortable feeling there was very little preventing his refusing outright. What little there was consisted of Jackson's Baker-Street-Irregular, Sherlockian-world general standing – and his house when Twatchel wanted to visit the Pleasant Valley scion, and be accommodated without having to pay room and board.

It was impossible to describe the man as mean, but where money was concerned he might be called careful. Clootie was not typical of the Washington male.

He was not gregarious (except amongst other Sherlockians). He did not (to Jackson's knowledge) frequent singles bars. He did not write the President's speeches, nor produce Senators' breakfasts, nor run their errands, nor collect their laundry, nor work for the

CIA. All of which, in Washington, made him more than unique: it made him an extinct species. Twatchel sat somewhere in the labyrinth of the Pentagon, planning wars.

"You've never been able to look after yourself!" Down the telephone, Jackson had persisted. "Look at that time you set fire to the freezer!"

"I was only trying to defrost it."

"With an electric heater? And tell me when was the last time you cooked yourself a meal?"

"I always –"

"I won't accept Graham Crackers!"

There had been an uneasy hush, in which it was possible to hear the churning of tapes.

"You need a housekeeper, Twatchel, you need someone to look after you!"

"My mother used to look after me. I couldn't stand it."

Jackson had shaken the receiver furiously, like a rattle. "This wouldn't be like a mother, this'd be more like –" He noticed Mercy, watching him round a club sandwich. "More like a sister. More like a *younger* sister, Twatchel."

"Oh my God she'll have that music on all the time."

"No she won't!"

"How d'you know? And if she's so wonderful, why don't you have her?"

"Because I'm having a friend of hers. I'm having Mercy." Jackson rubbed his stomach, which was diminishing remarkably, what with the exercise. "That's what gave me the whole idea. I'm happy – and I want *you* to be happy, Twatchel. And I happen to know the girl wants to see Washington."

"Why?"

"*Why*? *Why*?" Jackson made beseeching motions at Mercy, who was dumbstruck by lettuce and bacon. "Because – because she's never seen it, that's why."

"What'd she want to come down to this swamp for? Oh my God, do you realise what the temperature here today is? Have you told her we have ninety per cent humidity? Aw, tell her the truth, Jackson, we have ninety-nine per cent. Doesn't the term humidity mean anything to her? Tell her my jotter right here on my desk right now is sweating. What is this girl, a masochist or a mosquito?"

"Stop exaggerating!"

"Aw, no –"

"She wants to see Washington, and she can keep house, and you need a housekeeper! You can't deny it, you need a housekeeper, Twatchel. The last time I visited you there was green mould growing up the shower curtain! And I opened a bread-bin and there was a loaf of bread in there that had *hair*."

"Aw, well, I'm sorry –"

"Wouldn't you like to come home in the evenings to a clean house?"

"I don't care whether it's clean. I just like it empty."

This had been followed by twenty-four hours of stalemate.

Little things happened around the place in Society Hill. Cordelia failed, again, to get on the Board of the Art Museum. Kegan had a hangover and put all his patients on a whole-grain diet. Cordelia was outvoted as Chairperson on another Committee, and left her Mercedes stalled across two traffic lanes in Logan Circle. Mercy had the curse, cried and dropped things and was introduced by Jackson to polythene sheeting. And Jackson telephoned Twatchel Clootie again. And pointed out that Grace could surely stay with him while she looked round for work somewhere else in the city. In Washington, there would always be work for someone willing to clean up.

The silences which had initially contained Twatchel's refusals now began to contain nothing but silences. Three days later he relented. Jackson left a note for Grace at the hotel.

Grace left a note for the Personal Manager under his pillow – and told the YWCA Residence Director that her life-goals had opened out consideraly, and shifted south. She gave Beatrice a three-pound box of Continental chocolates (given her by a traveller in confectionery with only half a pound eaten) and the various colognes and perfumes she kept for herself.

In his note, Jackson had promised that Mercy would write to the Hopefuls, explaining, and that he would see the letter was posted in the right place.

And Jackson went to Thirtieth Street Station with Mercy, to buy the ticket and to see Grace off on a Metroliner. The plans had been set in motion. Jackson's. And Mercy's. And Grace's.

Part Four

All the rivers run into the sea; yet the sea is not full; unto the place from whence the rivers come, thither they return again.

XIV

The settlement stood, patient and white on its plain green acreage. The buggy waited in its shed and the mare mouthed the flowers in her paddock. The hens scratched and clucked in the sandy, pale yard beyond the gravel and a breeze stirred the leaves in the orchard. On the clothes-line billowed the long blue garments of the Eldresses, and their large, plain sheets, and their table-cloths and their coarse towels. The Maytag washing machine hubbled on the cobbles of the summer kitchen, and the flat irons stood heating, and the starch turned the water moony.

On one of the walls in the Eldresses' Meeting Room hung a new sampler – "*Bake Hopefully, mend Hopefully, make Hopefully, and count thy Change*" – worked in blue cross-stitching on bleached linen by little Titty.

In the airy closets, the bright quilts lay folded and covered, ready for trading. On the shelves in the still rooms, loaves of bread, and cakes, and pies were cooling. Jars of preserves gleamed beside the crocks of pickled eggs. The cheeses loomed, shrouded dully in muslin. Across the silence edged the creaking of the butter-churn.

Upstairs, every table, every chest, every chair-back glowed golden with wax polish, and the wood-block flooring reflected every foot that trod on it.

The scent within the house was of the dried petals that the Eldresses sewed into sachets for sale and for their own closets, and of the dried herbs that hung in the store-rooms, and of the baking. The scent was always fresh, for air moved through the house continually; it had been plainly built, but well, for ventilation, with transoms that could be readily opened, and vent holes in the baseboards.

The air stirred the white blinds at the large windows, so their wooden edges tapped gently on the glass panes. And the glass panes showed every green stretch of the glorious June in the settlement.

Another June, another summer. . . . In the Reading Room, the yellowed pages of the books grew infinitesimally more yellow. And Mother Germaine set down the single letter she had received from Mercy.

XV

Mercy slept most of the way up to Pleasant Valley. Jackson had collected his car from the long-term parking spot (where he'd left it rather than leave it where Cordelia might get it – right out there, exposed to her Mercedes on the street) and they had set off one early afternoon, while both Hiscock Mincham Muschamps were out about their own business, and Mercy was supposed to be freezing fresh vegetables that someone well-meaning had given Cordelia the night before.

"I can't do it!" Mercy had wailed pitifully to Jackson. "I can't put those poor things in that awful cold place!"

Mercy was convinced that freezing vegetables was sinful; she wasn't at all sure what happened to squash and tomatoes, or whether egg-plants had souls.

So it was in every way a suitable juncture, and rather than go through a whole lot of unpleasant argument Jackson had written a flowery, insincere letter and left a cheque in respect of one month of Mercy's wages and personally frozen the egg-plants. And, holding hands and their light respective baggage, they had taken a cab to the long-term car parking lot. And Jackson had stopped at a gas station and started off on the long drive north.

Mercy did not like the gas stations. Nor did she like the Highways. She sat shivering with terror, no matter how carefully and gently Jackson drove, and covered her eyes, and gave little wharbling cries as other vehicles muscled past them, and was in just about every aspect the most unnerving passenger he'd had since Sylvia, who had spent every journey of any length with him convinced she'd miscarry.

"But you're not pregnant!" he'd rave, driven out of his mind on some Freeway. And all Sylvia would do would be to clutch her abdomen and say darkly, "How do we know?"

Jackson knew. Jackson knew she was never pregnant. Sylvia took so many precautions against pregnancy she had no strength left over for sex.

If he allowed himself to think about it all now, his eyes grew misty. If anyone had borne him children, he would so much have liked it to have been this child. . . . His angel blonde moaned horribly as Lincolns and Volvos and even Rabbits droned past them.

But she was, after all, not much more than a child herself. Perhaps he could sublimate his paternal feelings by buying her candy? His knuckles whitened on the steering wheel. Oh God, how *stupid* to have had that vasectomy! What had he thought he was doing? What had he thought he was proving? He must have been drunk – yes, certainly he'd been drunk at the time. Perhaps he could have the operation reversed – you read about that. And you read about women having quads, after they'd been sterilised. He'd have a talk with his doctor – yes, that's what he'd do, he'd have a talk with his doctor.

Mercy said faintly, "Please, I want to be sick."

But Jackson couldn't find anywhere to pull in, in time.

When they resumed their travels, he found himself not quite so keen on children. There were their illnesses, weren't there, and diapers, and they threw up a lot.

He wound down a window.

And they'd be forever toddling in the bedroom just when he'd got Mercy ooo-ing and clawing on the brink of the kittens. And she wouldn't be so snug. And women lost their figures after they had children.

He glanced quickly at the honey bundle beside him (Mercy had wept herself to sleep).

Then again there were women who lost their figures anyway. And then again there were women who'd never had figures in the first place.

Mercy slept, incredibly, as far as the Taconic Parkway. When she roused, and whimpered, and struggled in her seat-belt, Jackson said softly, "We're nearly home." And he wished she could see around her, when they got on to the side roads, the rises and dips of the country, and the beauty of it all, and the dogwood trees. But all she could see were the phantom shapes of the trunks and branches in the darkness, and the mail-boxes and fence-posts, and the headlights, until eventually he slowed, and *slowed*, and veered into his driveway.

She was still so sleepy that he had to help her out of her seat and virtually carry her, and he set her down on the front porch, and fiddled for his keys, and let her into the hallway that smelled fusty with having been so long locked up, but still warm and sweet with books and wood and polish, and she said, "Oooo, Jackson," very nervous, and he said "We're home, darling. Here we are."

Part Five

Nineveh: Woe to the bloody city! it is all full of lies and robbery.

XVI

Grace had armed herself with a copy of *Playgirl*, and studied it as she bore down on Washington. That was when she wasn't being talked at, by the Philadelphia businessman in the next seat. He leaned so close she hoped he wouldn't crush her new uncrushable coffee co-ordinates. That was what the salesgirl had called them. She had also tried to sell Grace an under-slip. How stupid, when the material was so pretty transparent. The businessman talked to her about the corruption and the Mayor and the corruption, and the police department and the education system and the corruption, and the newspapers and the strikes and the corruption, and the fact it wasn't safe to walk around in Philadelphia alone now, at any hour of the day or night. And then he gave her his Washington telephone number, and said why didn't they meet for a drink tomorrow evening. He smelled of the gritty stuff men used to clean their dental plates.

Grace smiled at him, because she always smiled, in case it was useful, and said of course she would be pleased to have his number, but she was being met. And when he went to the men's room she swayed down the aisle but found nothing more comely, so she returned to her seat and resigned herself to having to hear him.

He pointed out Baltimore, as though she was liable to miss it, and Grace thought it was probably the ugliest sight she'd ever seen in her life.

Then as the time went by he pointed out the increasingly lush, wooded country, as though she mightn't have noticed it was different after Baltimore.

And eventually he pointed out they were arriving in Washington. It seemed to Grace she was twenty-five years older than she'd been when she got on the train.

Because he was being met too, he said, he didn't help her with her baggage (she had been to Wanamakers and bought a valise). And they stepped out of the train as though they were strangers, although he had spent the last couple of hours pressed very close to her, and Grace watched him disappearing in the crowds and wrinkled her pretty nose at his suit back; the last few weeks in the hotel had taught her all about him.

The waiting area after she walked in from the tracks was clean and lit strangely – not brightly, but the light made everyone look sallow, and left no shadows. Opposite her was a rank of telephones and around were little nooks, with low seating, where people stared at the floor, and their clasped hands, and their squabbling children, as though these items might belong to someone else, if they were lucky. A very tall, very thin man in a very pale suit unfolded himself from a kind of footstool and came over through the surge of arrivals and said miserably, "You're Grace."

"Yes," she said. "Are thou Mr Clootie?"

A hunted expression; he seemed to be wondering if there was some way he could deny it. "Did Jackson say you could call me Mr Clootie or Twatchel?"

"No." She shook her head, and Mr Clootie winced. "He didn't say."

Other travellers, and families and friends, and waving hands, milled all around them. The weight of the decision was obviously too much for Mr Clootie.

"If I'm going to be keeping house for thee, shouldn't I call thee –"

"You're not keeping house, you're rooming! Call me Twatchel." He fought away two matrons who were moving him too close to Grace in the mob. "You had a good journey." And, not waiting for a possibly distressing reply: "We go this way."

He made no attempt to take Grace's heavy valise from her; perhaps he didn't see it, because it was such a long way from his eyes, right down there at her feet. And he loped ahead of her now, a galloping seersucker hairpin, his long thin legs carrying him off so fast it was difficult for her to keep up with him. Occasionally, he pointed out a landmark. His voice carried back to her over the broad weave of the heads between them.

A brisk walk to the right, and they passed a row of ticket windows, and a kiosk in the middle of the hall – "Kiosk," called Twatchel Clootie. And, tucked in a corner, a funny, old-fashioned-looking railroad car – "That's a bar." The railroad car was full of relaxed, bulky policemen.

Through glass doors, up and along a ramp and into an enormous, carpeted chamber, and music floated around them from somewhere invisible, out of the air. Grace tried to look about and see everything, but it was hard doing that and hauling her valise, and listening, and not losing Twatchel Clootie. There were huge tubs of flowers and a restaurant – "Restaurant" – and information desks – "Information desks." There were wooden surfaces and sides to the desks, and a lot of what looked like sacking, but the walls were pretty – painted white and blue. Grace was by now almost running to keep within a fair distance of Twatchel, who didn't seem to be aware at all that he was moving very fast indeed. She hurried behind him into the main hall, and stopped short at the sight of a great oval pit. The sides of the pit were flickering with a motion picture, and great letters spelled out "Welcome to Washington" but she couldn't stay to see the show, Mr Clootie was vanishing among the people. Over towards the left there was a band seated on tiny chairs and playing – so that was the music – and around the hall were draped so many flags. . . .

She dragged her valise out of the station, and the heat hit her. Physically.

A physical blow to her body. The heat seized and swallowed her strength.

Twatchel was stooped with care, waiting, ready to gather his limbs and move again as soon as he saw Grace. "I'm parked in Columbus Plaza!" he yelped, before she could reach him, and hunched his shoulders wretchedly and strode off again.

If she was supposed to follow him, she didn't care. She staged a rebellion. She set down her valise and sat on it, and stared around, and panted for breath. The summers had been sweet and hot as long as she could remember, and whenever she wasn't caught and chastised and prevented she had splashed naked in the narrow creek beyond the orchard – or, if not naked, then only in her shift and her cotton drawers. But *this* – how did anyone breathe in this heat? It was like trying to breathe under water – very hot greasy water. Her co-ordinated coffee skirt was sticking to her thighs and her hair itched and prickled on her scalp. And this after only a minute – what would it be like to walk in this city? And it was evening now – how hot could it be at midday?

Yet, sitting there on her suitcase and sweating, Grace was still gradually affected by the sight before her. The utter flat blue of the sky, solid. And the brightness of the sunlight, even at this hour, glinting on the golden eagles that topped the tall white poles outside the station. And ahead of her, dazzling, seen between the poles and the trees and the visitors taking photographs, the high rounded dome out of all the pictures – the dome she had pursed her lips at, snapping through books on Washington for information in the bookstores on Chestnut Street. It was less hulking, more delicate than she had imagined. Its inset columns and arches fascinated her, like an incredible piece of immense white jewellery. Here she was, sitting on a suitcase in her co-ordinates, looking at the Capitol. She, Grace, recently of the Hopeful settlement. Most lately of Philadelphia and the cleaning trolley. Jackson had bought the ticket, but *she* had got here. She had got to Washington. She – .

"Aw, I didn't know where you'd got to!" The pale, frowning bent form of Twatchel Clootie, suddenly between her and the sunlight. "I'm parked in Columbus Plaza!"

Twatchel looked peevish. Awkward. Put upon by circumstances. He could have been one of those husbands Grace had seen on television quiz shows, shown up by their wives and bearing it for the sake of a new refrigerator. A thought appeared to come to him. She saw it come.

"Anything wrong with you?" It wasn't so much care, in fact it wasn't care one bit. It was clearly dread.

"It's hot and I'm hot and my case is heavy!"

She saw a tall thin man who acted as if his feet were eating him.

And Twatchel Clootie saw a young redheaded girl with frightening eyes and thin clothes on, and a lower lip that was out far too far for comfort. Jackson had been right – she was like a younger sister. The younger sister he'd always been so glad he didn't have.

"Can't you manage your case then?"

"No."

It took him quite a while to work out what to do. Finally he said, "I'd better take it for you?" and when Grace immediately stood up to let him, he gazed at her in a mixture of alarm and disbelief.

But thus, reluctantly and ungraciously, the two of them became a couple, and strode and trailed respectively towards the car. Twatchel dragged a door of it open – his door – threw her case in the back and then reached across to open a door for her. Grace tried to sit in the car, and cowered and shrieked.

"The seats are hot," said Twatchel unnecessarily. "The air-conditioning's broken."

Grace hated him deeply by this time. She lowered herself on the very edge of her seat and blew on her burns. Those that in public she could blow on. She'd noticed how he'd thrown her valise in the back seat upside-down, so probably her cologne would be broken and spilled and all her dresses would be ruined – she loathed him.

And he didn't wait for her to find both sides of her seat belt. He told her she had to put it on, but he didn't help her and he didn't tell her how. He said, "I suppose you might like to see a bit of Washington." He said this looking out of the window, and he said it hopelessly. He drove her around, saying what this building and that was, and pointing. Though, because he never actually stopped except at the lights, she got confused about what she was seeing. This Museum and that Museum, the National Gallery of Art, the Smithsonian, the Library of Congress, the National Museum of Natural History – as soon as he'd told her the long name of what was coming, it had gone. And all of them were vast, imposing buildings, usually with columns. Washington had more columns than a Sunday news-sheet. The White House was pretty, though, and dainty, away behind railings and gardens. Apart from the Capitol, it was the only place she recognised.

They passed a great tall shaft with a pointed top and a lot of people sitting around the bottom, and all the roads they drove along were avenues and boulevards. And all the sidewalks were so wide, and all the roadways were so wide, and all the vistas and views and sights were arranged to be breathtaking, and if she only could have breathed – if there had been any air for her to breathe with – she was sure her breath would have been completely taken away.

It was as white and as clean and as green and as open and as lovely as a picture in a magazine that said how life was better and sexier and shorter if you smoked cigarettes.

And the whitest and most open and loveliest of all was the Jefferson Memorial. It shimmered across the blue waters of the Tidal Basin, as soft as though it had been built of fresh snow. A shallow dome, a sort of lintel, and of course the columns. Facing out across the brimming, dull-glossy Basin. But its shape was so gentle, it wasn't vast or awesome at all. People should have been smiling there, and dancing in and out of it, and touching each-other's hands, and slipping down into the water, and having some Recreation. Grace said as much, forgetting her sweat and her sulks and actually speaking to the loathsome Twatchel Clootie, and Twatchel stared at her instead of staring out through the windscreen and said, "Could you see *The Ear* in Philadelphia?"

XVII

Twatchel was still muttering about *The Ear* being the gossip feature in the *Washington Star*, and what sort of scandal it printed, when they shuddered to a stop and peeled themselves off their seats in Foggy Bottom. He was becoming, if possible, even more boring when he talked than when he didn't. And he took such a very long time over everything – everything to do with words, not to do with walking. He was unstuck and locked up and walking away pretty quickly, and Grace's valise was still in the back seat of the car. He was leaving her there!

"Aw – yes," he admitted, shrilled and stamped at with tired and crumpled irritation from the other side of the red-hot vehicle, and he returned to haul on the ill-used luggage, and shuffle the document case already under one arm.

"Through here?" And he looked at her, as though there were some chance she could suggest an alternative. But she couldn't; if she could have done, she would have. "Through here" was a path between tangles of long grass, up a step off the sidewalk. Looking to right and left she could see that no-one else's grass was grown long and messy like that. The whole street was lined with hedges and prettily-coloured, prettily-shuttered houses, soft greens and soft golds, and mellow brickwork, and white. The next-door house to Twatchel's on one side had a trellis and two trees and a rose-bush, and the next-door house on the other side had no trellis but one tree and some shrubs. All of that going on in the small space of ground in front of the front doors. Twatchel's front yard didn't have too much in it – just grass, but the grass was waist-high. Against the house-wall crawled a vicious-looking creeper.

Grace had the feeling there might be shutters under there.

They stood in the twilight while Twatchel fumbled for his latch key, and then he shouldered open the door and hunched through with the cases, and let the door slap shut in Grace's face. Grace hollered "God damn thee!" and hammered with her fists and tore at her hair-style, and was found out in these actions by the bemused Twatchel Clootie, who finally remembered to turn around again and let her in. He gaped down at her as she flung herself past him, and her rage carried her into the depth of the house.

The tide of temper ebbed within ten or twelve paces, slackened by the impact of the first room. She halted, shaking, in the sudden dusk that had descended upon her; she was surely inside the dingiest dump in Washington.

* * *

At first she was only conscious that a certain haziness lay over everything. It was several minutes before she realised the haze was dust. And then it was hard to see all the dirt straight away, because the place was so untidy. Stacks of papers and books were on all the seats of the chairs and along the couch cushions, stacks more stood about the floor, papers and letters lay scattered over all the surfaces, and draped down in fans and streamers from the mantelpiece. A bowl of dead flowers squatted on a table, beside two full ashtrays and a plate smeared with dried egg. The room was dim, not just because of the twilight, but because the windows were so milky with filth they appeared to be curtained. In fact the curtains were pulled back, and hung limply in sooty-edged folds.

Pinned on the walls were a curious variety of objects – some, apparently, mementoes. Pictures and postcards and notes and – Grace started – *a long crimson rope*. Half of a wall had a curious stain on it, on another half the paper was peeling away. Twatchel threw down his document case, it hit a couch cushion and up flew a billow of dust.

They had passed through a hall so minute it had gone quite unnoticed, and were standing in what might loosely have been called a living room. "I've got this lower part of the house," said

Twatchel, with obvious relish. "The best of it. Two girls and a dog live upstairs."

Grace gazed at the ceiling. From it was coming a strange booming noise.

"Had it for years – ever since I came to Washington. It's convenient, and I've got the backyard." He sat down and a stack of books collapsed across him.

Grace swallowed. She said "Would thou mind if I looked around?"

"Aw, no. Help yourself." And Twatchel opened his case and his mail and forgot her. He read his documents silently, but his lips moved.

Grace buttoned herself up a little, just two buttons, and flexed her shoulders. At least in here the air-conditioning was working. The room was not only dirty, it was very cold. She wandered past the couch on which Clootie was seated, and absentmindedly let her hand slip over a chair. The chair-back felt furry. She looked down at her hand and saw it now bore a black smear.

Beyond the couch, towards the far end of the long room, was another table – a dining table, oval and set round with chairs. It, too, had a vase of dead flowers littered on it, and more ash-trays, but this time no plates. "I didn't notice thou smoked," she called back, moved to speak to Twatchel.

"What?"

"*I* didn't *notice* thou *smoked*!"

"Aw. I don't," he said. "Any more. I gave it up about four months ago."

To the side of the dining-area was an archway into a kitchen. She stood in the archway and, not just because of the temperature, froze. On every work-top were papers. Papers and papers and papers and papers. On the floor were several sacks full of empty loaf-wrappers and cookie cartons. But she was thirsty, and Twatchel had offered her nothing to drink. She teetered into the kitchen – the tiles were so gluey they nearly pulled her shoes off – and reached out tentatively for the door of the refrigerator. She tried to open it. And had to try harder. The door was stuck shut with something. When she got it open she saw it might have been spilled honey, or possibly yoghurt, or perhaps peanut butter. There was a choice. But there was nothing to drink.

There was an oven, though, and she was inquisitive. The oven appeared to have had something in it, once. When she unjammed that door, she saw that what it had had inside were cooking instructions. A nice-looking booklet, a bit charred round the edges, but apart from that. . . .

From the kitchen she could see down into the backyard – through the murky panes, just. Paving, being attacked by the lank grass. Lounging chairs and a table were dug in at angles. On the table was a tall jug and several glasses, and whatever was in the jug was the same colour as the stain on the living-room wall.

Grace turned around and walked back out of the kitchen. She felt as though the way she was moving was funny, like those people on television before they use soap.

To her left now was another door, back into the tiny hallway, and from there she saw a narrow corridor leading off, lined with doors. Every door she tried to open was half stuck, but behind each was a cupboard. Most of what was in the cupboards came out hurriedly on to the floor.

At the end of the stretch of corridor was a bit of space with three more doors, and these were wider. A bathroom – the mirror was opaque. She walked over to the basin, and it had a thick coating of mousey hair. So had the vanity surround. So, when she pulled back the shower curtain, had the bath tub. The toilet, when she tried it, hiccupped but didn't flush.

The next door along the space was to a bedroom. It contained a stationery store after a typhoon, and an unmade bed. And clothes, which lay in interesting patterns over the carpet. As she trod on the carpet, it gave up little cloudy sighs of dust.

Back to the final door, and this led into a dark room. She felt her way around it, to the window. And drew back the curtains, choking, and forced open the casement, and pushed out a shutter (only one – one wouldn't go). Revealed, the room was a small second bedroom. It was also, she could see, used as a store-room. There were picture-frames, a bicycle, and five old clocks. Several hundred books, and a mountain of wire clothes-hangers. An iron on an ironing-board. And, under a heap of towels and suits and maps and cardboard boxes and dirty laundry, a bed.

She was staring at the mattress when Twatchel arrived in the doorway. He was holding two tall sticky glasses unhappily. Had he brought them in from the backyard? "I didn't know whether you'd want a cooler." From anybody else, this would have been an offer. From Twatchel Clootie, it came as an accusation. Then, "I see you found everything," on a note of utter misery.

Whatever the drink was, she took it from him, and followed him dumbly back to the living-room. Too stricken even to worry about her new coffee co-ordinates, she sank down on a stack of magazines as far from Twatchel as possible. What would the Phrasebook of Uplift have to say in a situation like this? This was one field that *was* too large for the Hopeful plough.

She sipped the drink – it was very sweet indeed – and found a few inches to leave the glass on, on the almost invisible low table beside her.

"Aw –" An anxious sound. Twatchel was watching, looking fussed and awkward. "Aw – would you mind using a coaster? There's one there, see? Under the picture? Wet glasses depreciate the furniture."

Stiff-fingered, she lifted the glass again, seeking the coaster. Her drink had left a round basin in the grey dust.

XVIII

The worst of it took five days, and the first day was the worst.

For both of them.

Twatchel hunched back home to a war zone in which the only objects recognisable were his pictures, removed from amongst the other litter, graded according to size and resting against an unfamiliar, light-coloured wall.

He rushed to them, posters and prints, his document case thumping in anguish. "*Those*!" he screamed at her, "were *there*!" – waving a wild, undiscriminating, dramatic finger, "to *remind* me to have them *framed*!"

Grace merely looked at him. She was as filthy as the main room had been that morning, and even in the freezing air-conditioning her hotel coverall was soaked through with sweat. The monogram rose and fell on her breast pocket. "To remind thee," she repeated at last, as from a distance. "They were all around the place like that, in all of the rooms, just to remind thee."

"Yes!"

"But thou hasn't had them framed. One of them's got a ticket on it – a present from Mother, Christmas sixty-eight."

"Aw – I'd have gotten around to it! I'm a busy man! Now they're all stacked like that, how am I supposed to remember!"

She went away from him. He heard her in the bathroom. He heard her in the kitchen. He heard her in the recesses of the apartment. He heard the spare-room door close. And when he entered his own bedroom later he saw that she'd taken a squeeze bottle of chocolate flavoured dessert topping (it was still there, standing by the base-board) and written, "Remember to have thy pictures framed" in letters four feet high across a wall.

It was the last exchange they ever had about tidying or cleaning. Neither of them referred to the subject again.

Twatchel loped off to the Pentagon every morning before Grace left her bedroom, and returned in the evening to the sound of the shower running, and music pulsing from the radio beyond the wasteland created by bleach and foaming cleanser and detergent – the napalmed area. Grace, her stint of work over, and out of range of his vision, danced to the radio. Her slim, delicate, wet footprints shone from the bathroom and wove along the floors to her door. Twatchel, who noticed nothing, noticed that. The thought of her naked, undried eurhythmics aroused in him gloomy forebodings: she would catch cold and he might have to nurse her. There were other, even more dire possibilities. He began locking his door at night. The latch, long unused, made a loud sound which was always followed by the faint ripple of Grace's giggling from along the corridor space, through the walls.

She washed his underwear, too; he didn't like that. He put her intimate knowledge of his clothing out of his mind, but sometimes, in certain positions and situations, it came to him that her hands had touched and folded what he was wearing and the thought filled him with dread.

He attempted to hide his pants but she found them. If he were to remain sane in the purgatory created by this remorseless *female*, this embarrassingly mobile redhead – to whom nothing was sacred – he would have to rise above it. He just wished she would wear more beneath her own clothes. At least a brassiere. It would have been worse, of course, if he'd had to appear in public with her. That he'd quickly made clear was quite impossible. He had told her about the Metro, and told her where it was, and left it at that. Grace, he gathered, had found and entered Foggy Bottom Station. Between her and the tracks had stood the machine-run Metro Farecard system, which snatched dollar-bills out of the hands of would-be commuters and fed them back small oblongs of matte plastic. Grace had said that evening, over defrosted lasagne, that the Metro didn't go anywhere she wanted to go. From then on she stayed in the apartment, or she walked.

In some ways, small ways, things remained gratefully normal. His ceilings shook beneath the secretaries upstairs and their dachshund. When Friday night came he bought a box of pastries. Whatever the day, he brought documents home with him and read them – for hours, keeping Grace at bay ostentaciously. His 'phone rang and he answered it (when he knew where she was). Very much more rarely, he made a call. Over the weekend he typed reports on his portable, taking frequent breaks to ungum the keys. When he felt dispirited he concentrated on what he was doing: he was deeply glad about the Neutron bomb.

After six days, when he could see the strange, light colour of the paintwork everywhere, and sat down in clean underpants and shirts and pressed suits on clean surfaces, and couldn't find anything, he received a call for Grace. It was from Jackson, who didn't ask him – Twatchel – much of anything, and Grace came to the 'phone from the kitchen, smelling of bacon and coffee and odd, disturbing, indefinable scents. She had on a loose blouse, the kind girls wore over Levis, but she didn't have on any Levis or even shorts under it. She said "Yes, yes," and "Yes, thank thee," and "*Yes*!" and began to splutter, and moaned "Oh, that shower curtain!" and "I scoured the bread bin!" and curled up over the receiver, bare legs, a tiny edge of blue panties, the loose blouse, her tumbling head of red hair, laughing and choking for breath.

Twatchel slapped his documents together and went to his room to brood in his dignity. The sanity of solitude – but even that was less of a pleasure now that his books had been routed and the invasion had passed over his coverlet and tucked in his blankets and sheets. He had got to page eight of the dossier he was reading before he realised, pinned there helpless by his self-disgust, that he had actually removed his shoes before throwing himself down on his bed.

"Aw. Awwwww," groaned Twatchel. And he thrashed about on the heavy wool cubist design, his flailing hands and scissoring feet scattering his dossier, tears of rage oozing over his pale skin and running into his mousey hairline. "Awwwww, awwwwwwww!" What was happening to him? A half-hour later, still groaning to himself and weeping intermittently, he rose from his bed like a beaten gantry and awkwardly smoothed the covers again. Grace was still on the telephone.

The following evening, when he came home there were cling-wrapped sandwiches, made and left in the refrigerator for him. A pitcher of iced tea, and a dressed salad. And the booming ceilings. And she wasn't there.

* * *

Grace was sitting with a white wine spritzer in the garden at Hot Diggety Dog. She had asked for a long drink, and one that was cooling, and the waitress had brought her this tall glass of pearly bubbles that reached down inside her as she sipped it, down her arms and legs, and eased the aches in her muscles. It was five o'clock, and there was some air at last here outside, and she had a new journal, and her hair was washed, and she was wearing a fresh white-and-yellow dress. She turned her head so that the air reached round her neck, and when she had finished reading a piece of writing about eye-liners she ordered a second white wine spritzer. Then she read a glamorous illustrated story.

At about five-thirty she got into conversation with a black man in a very elegant suit who had sat at a nearby table with a newspaper and the same sort of glass she had and taken off his jacket.

At about six-thirty, when he'd taken everything else off and they were in the bathroom together, he told her he worked for the FBI. She didn't understand what that meant, she asked him what company was it, and he stopped soaping her and said it wasn't the Company, it was the FBI.

She pouted at him and asked again, and he wouldn't believe her, and then he believed her. And recited to her, rinsing, dull difficult phrases about the Department of Justice and the overall direction of the Attorney General, and the Bureau exercising police jurisdiction over all crimes not the special concern of the other federal agencies, and the Bureau handling the internal civil security of the United States.

He went to switch on some music and she heard him laughing and snorting; he seemed to find his work very funny. Just as he'd found it funny when she'd said wistfully how clean the rooms were – he'd said they ought to be, they were swept once a week, and he'd laughed at lot at that.

He had a firm, muscular body, on which he stretched her like an offering to someone not present. He hooked his feet round from inside her ankles, held her wrists in one hand and stretched her, taut, the whole length of him – her back against his chest, her thighs over his, his teeth meeting in the locks of hair behind her ears – caressing her till she rippled and struggled under his wide, exploring, inescapable free hand. He was only preparing her for himself, but she did not want to get off him. She wanted something more now. As well as. Someone else. *As well as*. Whispering and murmuring. She wondered what it would be like to be made love to by another man, while she was being held this way by this one. Perhaps, eventually, that would be how she could get to the sixth room without leaving the first.

He rolled from underneath her, and she opened her mouth under his, and she enjoyed him. But it was still the same room. A room full of silvery-coloured furniture, and music, and plants.

His name was Benjamin Williams and later she asked him if she could call him B.W. He was puzzled over that, shrugging into his Thai silk jacket. (She had touched it, and asked the material, and he had told her it was Thai silk.) Why initials? But she'd just been reading the magazine story and all the men in that were called by initials, so it must be fashionable and elegant, and finally he said she could if it pleased her. So to her then he became B.W.

He was quieter now, looking at her a lot, more as though he hadn't had her yet and wanted her very much, and he took her to dinner in Georgetown. They saw two cars blasting their horns at one-another across a parking space, and a girl leaned out of a little low car and screamed at the man facing her in the other automobile, "Yo' mutha wuz a hooka!"

And when he dropped her back outside the long grass in Foggy Bottom, he said "Here? Not with Twatchel Clootie?" And she said no, not with Twatchel Clootie.

And they sat in the wide, cushioned darkness and talked about Twatchel, who was a friend of a man who worked alongside B.W.

It seemed the FBI was quite big and quite busy, as well as being so funny. And it knew an awful lot about an awful lot of people. And it all went to show, despite outward appearances, what a very, very small place Washington was.

Over the weeks that followed, it became smaller and closer. Grace met the secretaries upstairs (Anne and Rose Mary) when they were trying to get in the house one early morning with two gentlemen they introduced as lobbyists. And a while after that she met them again, without the lobbyists but with headaches. And then she met them again, with their garbage and dachshund.

As a neighbourly gesture they took her to a bar with noise; they apologised for the mess in the Porsche. All three of them left separately – Grace with a slim, damp, generous man named John Roberts Jobsdock – and when Grace was telling B.W. a little but not entirely all about it next evening, he changed the subject and became even more quiet.

He was not the only one who was quiet with her lately. Twatchel had even stopped asking her when she was getting a job.

Whatever groceries and stuff she wanted, he paid for. She wrote out lists of what she needed and he drove to supermarkets and collected brimming paper sacks and left them defeatedly in the kitchen, and wrapped himself up in his document case. Showing obvious pain, he parted at the end of each week with a twenty dollar bill for her, and Jackson also sent occasional spending money, with inquisitive notes about her progress as a missionary. And B.W. took her to dinner and bought her books and jewellery and shoes and perfume. It was an untroubled life, really. The only trouble was not getting to a sixth room any longer.

B.W. lay awake or sat in chairs half the nights she was with him, drinking vodka and switching on and off music and talking about that. He was the first man she had ever known for long enough and liked enough to talk to properly about it. He'd wanted her to, forced her to, but when he'd heard it weighed on him and pressed his shoulders down. He sweated, worked, fought both their bodies to be the sixth man for her – but scratching her pale limbs lightly, slightly, with his broad bluish fingernails, the whites of his curly-lashed eyes bloodshot, his breath dry, his soft lips pressed together and then drawn back, mauve, against his heavy perfect teeth, he told he that he wouldn't touch her after other men had been with her, and she smiled sweetly at him and thanked her stars John Roberts Jobsdock had shown her how to use his bidet.

XIX

"How many fellows are you seeing, Grace?"

"None of thy business."

"D'you go out to those bars much? Meet many fellows there?"

"What does thou think I meet?" Her eyes were quite wicked. "I met thee, are thou complaining?"

His damp hands touched his tie briefly, adjusted his cuff-links. "Not at all. I just like to be reassured what a friendly little thing you are."

She gurgled into her wine glass, misting it from the inside. Some of the wine she was swallowing leaked back into the rest from her mouth. He pointed a butter knife at her. "That's disgusting."

He made her laugh. Everyone made her laugh, when she'd been drinking that much wine. He ordered quantities of wine, the French wine, for her. And between him and B.W. and Anne and Rose Mary she was getting to know the city. Steamy hot Washington.

Georgetown was where you ate, and it was fashionable and expensive. Dupont Circle was where you drove through, and it was bohemian and liberal (and that meant it was all right for it to be old and tacky). Foggy Bottom was where you lived and it was pretty and arty. Fourteenth Street had Archibald's Topless Dancing Girls. West of all these districts, or south, were the great big buildings with the columns. She'd begun to have a map of it, in her head.

The map extended a long way now, thanks to John Roberts Jobsdock. He worked in Government, whatever that meant, and he lived in a condominium out in Arlington, though it just looked like a whole lot of houses to Grace. And she couldn't tell where Washington stopped being Washington and started being Arlington, but it was a drive to John's place along a Highway and the signs said it was in Virginia. Sometimes, if he'd met her early and didn't want to drive back to the city, he took her to dinner in a funny, ugly little restaurant in Maclean (that was also Virginia) where the waiters were Oriental-looking and the food burned her mouth and they drank beer. It wasn't crowded when they went. He said it was crowded at lunch-times. He said everyone he'd ever worked with had been to lunch there.

She saw him once or twice a week. It depended on B.W.

If she went to the bars with Anne and Rose Mary, those were the nights she didn't see B.W. There wasn't time, and anyway she knew he would taste the men on her.

But John Roberts Jobsdock wore contact lenses and was fastidious and left no traces. He was of medium height, medium weight, medium build, and perspired a little. Whenever they parted she forgot what he looked like. Immediately. It was only his voice she remembered. He had a light, quick voice that came over as breathy on the telephone. He rang her often – just short calls – at Twatchel's, and when Twatchel was there he rattled his papers and chewed at the insides of his sunken cheeks. She had taken to patting Twatchel on the top of his head if he was seated as she passed him, and she passed him very often now, going to answer the telephone. He cringed but suffered it, and he wasn't really loathsome, she had decided, with the magnanimity of having housebroken him. He hairpinned about the apartment, a huge pale insect, pencils clenched in his teeth and wads of papers under his thin arms. She prepared food for him but they rarely ate it together. Mostly she would bounce out of her room on an air cushion of perfume and cooking instructions, and rush down the path to B.W.'s or John Jobsdock's car.

John passed away like a tasteless glass of tepid water. She could meet him for a drink or a talk or a meal or a trip to Arlington, and carry nothing of him on to B.W. It was almost as though he encouraged being forgettable – being untraceable. Not only because of his bidet – though that was a safety insurance.

There was nothing so pallid about B.W., in comparison. He took her with him to motion pictures and concerts. He took her to parties, and she met his friends. She had no idea whether there were such things as friends of John Roberts Jobsdock. But B.W. had them, plenty of them. And they were funny, about things that had been in the newspapers, or things that didn't get into the newspapers, or they were serious about books and music. Grace didn't always understand all of what they were saying, and B.W. translated it patiently for her. Or they translated themselves for her, laughing.

They drew her in among them, they were all over her – not because of the way she looked, not because of what she might do, but because of the way she spoke and because of where she came from. They asked her about the Hopefuls, they wanted to know the Society details, they listened to the sayings from the Phrasebook of Uplift, and some of them went into clusters and learned off the Phrases by heart. Chanted them, to whatever was on the stereo. They wanted to know about Mother Germaine and Sister Agatha and Sister Lorelei and Sister Unity and Sister Heloise and Sister Amy. Some of them planned hazy excursions to the settlement, till Grace explained they should only go there if they really wanted to become converts. They actually heard and understood about her having been sent out. They understood, and joked, because she wasn't going to go back. They called her a rotten red hot missionary. B.W. said she was his fallen angel. They laughed, but they did not laugh unkindly. One of them said, "If they don't have 'phones I could move in and finish my novel!" Another said "Well – it'll depend how the primaries go. . . ."

It would have been possible to live an entire life with B.W. Except that she didn't want to. It would have been easy – easier, in fact – to move in with him. But she didn't want to move in with anyone who held her that tightly. Who searched her face as though looks could leave marks.

Every pore of her skin had been watched in the Hopeful Society and she never wanted to be known that well again. The appearances and disappearances, the *invisibleness* in the hotel had been so perfect for her. She liked a life of jigsaw puzzle pieces, and she liked being the only one who knew how many pieces there were. She liked fitting the pieces into the days as it pleased her. She liked having as few as possible bothersome questions to answer.

Sometimes she thought about Mercy. Mercy, the purest and most blameless of all the Hopefuls. Being screwed senseless by that tubby, rather sexy looking man in Pleasant Valley. She wondered which of them was doing the most converting. And whether Jackson caught cold, the way Mercy cried over everything.

Sometimes Grace thought about the Hopeful settlement. And about the starchy Sisterhood.

But mostly she thought of what was to happen in each day as it opened before her. She was practical about the people she met – she enjoyed them nearly all. Of course she liked B.W. very much. But who was to know when she'd meet someone she liked even better, in Clyde's or Nathan's or The Third Edition, or any of those bars.

It was true she liked B.W.'s friends. A lot. But she also liked the friends of Twatchel Clootie, who came by his house and always said, "Sorry, I must have come to the wrong place," and stayed to talk about Sherlock Holmes in voices high with excitement, and then followed her in the backyard or the kitchen and said could they show her round. One of them took her to the Press Club, which was full of men with tall brown glasses and women with hats on, and she saw John Roberts Jobsdock at another table, and she grinned at him and wriggled her fingers, and he raised an eyebrow at her and gestured and caught a waiter, and the next time they were alone he told her what gregarious meant.

When she was by herself during the day in Foggy Bottom, and the housework was done, and B.W.'s books were too difficult, she would dip into one of Twatchel's Sherlock Holmes books. The stories were short, which was good, and they were old and set in England; she put rings round the words she didn't know; the stories were fantastic. Twatchel got upset about the rings but he spoke about Sherlock Holmes over pancakes, or pie, or salad, on the few occasions she spent an evening in, and he explained his length of crimson cord was because of *The Abbey Grange* story, so she wouldn't show him up by being ignorant in front of his fellow members of The Red Circle. He didn't seem to realise that, once on their own with Grace, the Sherlockians did not discuss the Master with her, they just ripped her clothes off. Grace had been relieved to find they were so normal. She hadn't liked to think that poor old Twatchel might have peculiar friends.

Mainly because of the time problem, though, she didn't see much of them. Just an afternoon or evening, here and there. The person she saw most of was B.W. Sometimes he got angry and sad and she thought he was tiresome, but usually he was nice and funny and enjoyable in bed and she liked being with him.

* * *

And then one night she saw John Jobsdock at a party she had gone to with B.W., and B.W. saw him too, and narrowed his lips beside her ear and murmured something dirty about the Company. B.W. was morose, and had been drinking, and spent the party blocking Grace off in a window seat corner, and telling her what a lot of conscienceless shits they were in the CIA. John watched them from across the room, out of the sides of his lenses. It was obvious the men knew one-another, but they didn't speak.

The following day John telephoned her and they had lunch together. He polished his cutlery on his napkin, drank two Martinis slowly, said he'd seen her the previous evening with Benjamin Williams, an interesting fellow, she had catholic tastes. . . .

And then said there was this guest – there was in Washington a guest of the Government. A foreigner. Knew nobody. Very lonely. He was approaching her because she was such a pleasant girl, such a good mixer, friendly and outgoing, sensible naturally, and they wanted this man, this important guest, to receive the best impression of America. Particularly, of American hospitality.

Grace ate her Chef's Salad.

It would be fun. And an honour for her – representing America to a stranger.

She noticed the simple design of his cuff-links. Funny, she always noticed them and then forgot them, as she forgot him, afterwards. The cuff-links and John – they were so simple you couldn't remember them.

There would – he touched a little flower bowl – there would be a great deal of money in it for her. She would be this important man's – paid companion. Tour guide – if that was what he wanted. She would also have to help him with his English.

Grace chewed daintily at her chicken, and then said, "I'm not moving out of Twatchel's apartment. I've got it straight now." She was the redhead who hadn't ever given up her YWCA room, not in all the time in Philadelphia.

"You wouldn't need to move, just so long as you understand you wouldn't always be able to get back home – suppose you were away for a weekend – you might not be able to get back there every night." His lenses glinted. "That won't be any change, will it. I'm sure Twatchel Clootie is very accommodating. You aren't there every night, are you."

"I'm not anywhere every night. I like seeing lots of people. I like seeing thee. I like seeing B.W."

"B.W.?"

"Benjamin Williams."

The name caused a break in the conversation. There was an adjustment to the cuff-links. John hadn't appreciated, he said when he continued, the full extent of the relationship.

Grace had an appetite. She finished her salad and looked around, smiling delightedly, and said wasn't this the place with the gorgeous desserts.

* * *

It took a couple of days for John Roberts Jobsdock to decide it didn't matter, that perhaps her friendship with B.W. was not – he had sounded almost amused over the telephone – such a bad thing after all. During these days Grace hadn't heard from B.W. anyway. He was probably sitting around with his music and his vodka, talking about the sixth room all by himself. She grew bored. And Twatchel unexpectedly tried to be helpful. He told her more about Sherlock Holmes and loaned her a copy of *The Pentagon News*.

At a bar with noise and Anne and Rose Mary, Grace met a member of the Israeli legation, and Rose Mary borrowed her perfume and told her in the ladies room that Hitler had been jealous of the Jews because of their incredible sex drive. Grace went home with the member of the Israeli legation, who had an erection all night which would not go away whatever happened. He could also make marvellous coffee and scrambled eggs and was a very nice person, but in the morning what had been the first room was still the first room.

On Friday John 'phoned and gave her the address of an apartment in the Potomac Plaza. The guest of the Government was a Mr Saetiger and he was looking forward to meeting her Monday.

That weekend she saw B.W. again and they talked of nothing troublesome or important. They didn't get out of bed till half an hour before their table booking, and she sat in the candlelight, eating her dinner, with the marks of his teeth purple on her bare shoulders.

On Sunday she found him crying silently, and went out and caught a cab back to the house in Foggy Bottom. He 'phoned her later and said he must have been drinking too much, and she told him she'd washed her hair.

On Monday she went to meet Mr Saetiger. The guest of the Government. He was tall and solidly built, like a brick building, and his face was the colour of old bricks, too, and his hair was cut very short and was very stiff and bristly. He had small, square teeth, tobacco stained, and a battered, shapeless ring on his left hand, and a very new looking suit he didn't seem happy in, and he smelled of cigar smoke.

He was polite and watchful, and offered her coffee. He filled the soundless apartment as though the large rooms did not fit him. His name was Semyon (he spelled it out for her), and when he was making love to her, he groaned. He examined himself afterwards, tenderly. He said, "Have not make love, long time," and frowned over his foreskin, wincing as he eased it back and forward.

Grace lay quietly, folding her hands on her stomach, wondering whether she could get hold of the Israeli member.

And John Roberts Jobsdock. And one or two of Twatchel's Sherlock Holmes friends.

But, however she thought over it, she could only see herself getting hold of five people. *Damn* that she couldn't go to B.W. *Damn* him. *Damn* him.

There was always the telephone number, though. The number of the Philadelphia hotel guest – she hadn't bothered to call him yet. She could do that. If she hurried.

She got up to go and Semyon said, "You come back this evening?"

And Grace sat down on the bed again, and said slowly "Well – that might be an idea. If I came back to see thee. . . ."

And in the early hours of Tuesday morning, nearly fourteen hours after he'd first opened the door to her, Grace howled and clung in the bricklike arms of the solid guest of the Government, and got what she'd been wanting ever since the beginning in the hotel in Philadelphia – the finding of the sixth room right there in the very first room.

Part Six

The mountain of myrrh, and the hill of frankincense.

XX

Mercy rested her needle a moment, and said, "Jackson, dearest, what are Peas Eebees?"

"Uh?"

"Peas Eebees, Jackson dearest. There were some ladies talking about them outside the supermarket. Are they kinds of sodas no-one likes very much? One lady was saying what would they do when they ran out of Seven Up."

Jackson dragged his attention from the Phrasebook of Uplift. It pleased Mercy if he read the Phrases, and the Phrases gave him inordinate pleasure. "*A Hopeful woman carries the yoke through life*," he would declaim, "*and a Hopeful man carries the bridle*!" before seizing Mercy and throwing her on the hearthrug.

"Peas Eebees? The supermarket?" He had driven Mercy down to Pleasant Valley that afternoon, to get the shopping. Mercy would not actually go in the supermarket with him – she stood outside or cowered in the car. But she liked to accompany him everywhere. Everywhere that wasn't too big, or too noisy, or didn't have too many people.

"Peas Eebees. . . . Peas Eebees. . . . PCBs! PCBs are something we've got in the drinking water. They reckon if you drink the Hudson River water till you're seventy, you may very well drop dead of the PCBs."

"Ooooo –"

"That's if you haven't been hit by a truck or a skateboard. Or suffered a coronary." Jackson reached over and poked at her thigh with the Phrasebook. "I don't think you should start taxing your mind with carcinogens. The day you know about carcinogens will be the same day you stop doing *everything*."

But Mercy went and fetched a glass of water, and studied it under the bright light of his reading lamp. "I can't *see* anything," she said finally.

"That's good."

"They're not like fish, then?"

"No."

"And thee can't taste them when thee swallows them?"

"No."

She bit her lip, but she trotted off to empty away the water, and obediently returned to her mending. It seemed unnatural and almost obscene, Jackson thought fondly, watching her, that such a glorious little creature should be so industrious.

"Thee likes the Phrasebook, doesn't thee?" The needle winked in and out of the worn material; she was putting patches on the elbows of his favourite old jacket.

Sylvia would never have done that. She used to throw his clothes out. She never had understood the ritual or the sympathetic magic that surrounded all his writing – the special, comfortable, worn out clothes he got into, the box files for reference by his feet, and the dictionaries. His inability to start working without a spare typewriter ribbon, and a pencil sharpener, and a pair of scissors.

"Yes, I do like it." And I like this: this evening, watching you.

"Thee can see why I couldn't ever, ever be anything else but Hopeful."

"Yes, I can see that." He could see the shirring around the neckline of her apricot coloured blouse, and the shirring in the waist of her darker apricot skirt. She was sitting with one foot tucked up under her – a white ankle bone, a high instep, a rosy sole, pearly toenails. Her other foot dangled, the toes just tickling the rug.

The beauty of it, the richness of the cosy feeling it gave him, to sit in the long, mellow room with its wood floors and its bookshelves and its lamps and its overstuffed chairs. To have eaten the aromatic, delicious food she cooked him. To know that here was no scheming emasculator.

"Dearest?"

"Yes."

"Does thee think it would be nice to take a holiday from these Peas Eebee things?"

His head jerked slightly. He looked surprisedly at her. She was intent on her sewing.

"Thee doesn't think thee's been swallowing too many of them? Thy poor insides –"

"Insides? Holiday? We've only been back here a few weeks – I'm supposed to turn in the manuscript September 1st and I'm still researching!"

The patch troubled her for a while. It obviously required close, careful stitches. She said, "So we couldn't go for a little visit to the settlement?"

Jackson gulped. For the first time since he'd set eyes on her, Mercy had created a distinctly hollow sensation in the area beneath his zipper. "A little visit? All the way back down to Pennsylvania? If you want to visit anywhere, let's go to New York."

"Ooooo –"

"All right, Mercy! There, there. It's all right, calm down, I didn't mean it."

"Ooooo – thee's teasing me! Thee's being reckless and drinking all those terrible Peas Eebees – but I'm not brave like thee. I don't want thee to die when thee's only seventy!"

"I won't, don't worry. We have our own well water up here, Mercy, I should have explained to you, we don't have a problem." He was wrong; they had a problem.

"And I only wanted to go and see the settlement with thee before winter sets in."

"Winter? This is August!"

"I know, and it's hot, and thee'd feel much cooler in the settlement."

Jackson removed her mending and took her on his knee and drew her a map on his scrap-pad. "The settlement, Mercy, do you see, is right down south of here. We're up here, do you see? We are north, so we're cooler. If you go down to Pennsylvania, it gets hotter. If you go down here, to Washington, you broil."

"Ooooo, poor Grace!"

"Grace sounded absolutely fine last time I spoke to her. She's found lots of friends and she said she was enjoying herself. Twatchel seemed a bit low, but that's about what I expected – I wouldn't like to be a war planner and come up against a Hopeful. But you do see, Mercy, we are cooler here."

"No, we're not, dearest. It's ever so hot and it was always so cool in the settlement." This, though she would have gone on the rack rather than admit it, was nothing more nor less than a downright lie. In the summer heat, in their long starched dresses, they had often sweltered in the settlement. On certain days only the still rooms and the summer kitchen had been bearable. Grace was known to have bathed completely undressed in the creek.

"Mercy, this is one of the coolest houses I've ever been in! It stands up here with this ground and this view –" His arm made an arc towards the darkened windows, beyond which occasional lights twinkled on the other distant hillsides. "We get all the air there is going."

"It's so busy here." Trying another tack – she was fiddling with one of his buttons.

"*Busy*! Mercy, the only place less busy than this would be a shack in the Adirondacks. Sylvia used to lie around chewing and saying Pleasant Valley ought to have a sign up, warning people to be quiet in the exhibition! She used to say the only thing going on was the trees growing, and they were moving closer to the house. She used to say all that green stuff out there was taking over. She may not have walked out because of a deerstalker or a rack of pipes, she may have walked out because she wanted to see more action! She told me she wanted to see more life – 'Life, life, life, not a waxworks!' – that's what she told me. As far as I know she's seeing life in every urban connovation between here and the West Coast. If he's got any sense, Mr Goodbar is looking for *her*!"

Mercy moved on to a lower button and said, "I don't understand thee."

"No, of course you don't. What I mean is, this house and this place and this whole area aren't what anyone could call *busy*. Didn't you see the graffiti on that wall last weekend – 'I wanted to commit suicide but in Poughkeepsie death is redundant'?"

"I saw it, but I didn't understand it." Mercy was working on three buttons now. "The town and the markets and all of that – they seem busy to me."

"Town? Which town, Mercy? I've driven you into Pleasant Valley and I've driven you into Poughkeepsie. I've driven you to the supermarkets. I've driven you through Millbrook and, God help me, Wappinger. I wouldn't like to compare any of it to Columbus Circle."

Mercy pouted.

"That's in New York and it's all right, I know you don't want to go there. Look – do you want to get married, Mercy?" This, in Jackson's distant experience, had usually been the reason for a girl to start talking nonsense or finding fault with an ideal situation. Sylvia had been the last and best at this referred-pain technique, emerging with a bouquet and an empty victory, but he thought he could still recognise the syndrome, even though twenty-five years and a lot of behavioural guidance manuals had drifted under his marital mattress since then.

But his question didn't get at the root of what was bothering Mercy. She dropped his buttons. She wrinkled her brow at him: he was trying to change the subject. "Jackson dearest, in the eyes of the Lord we are already married."

Foolish. Conventional. Jackson was made to feel absurdly like a high school virgin. If there were such an animal. He seemed to remember they had been rare even in his early youth.

"The Hopefuls accept that outside thee has celebrations for marriages, but in the Society we don't believe in pomp, and ceremonial. That kind of–" She frowned, and her hands smoothed his collar. "That's the Worldly trappings of popery."

"So what do you do when you – um, when you want to – ah, set up home together?"

"Well, I don't know exactly because it's never happened in my lifetime." Mercy wriggled about, and Jackson tried to keep his mind on what she was saying. "There've always been just the Eldresses and Grace and Titty and me, and poor old Brother Orville. Oh, poor –"

"Yes, I know, poor old Brother Orville. But weren't there ever any –" He fumbled awkwardly for an expression. "Weren't there ever any Elders to *match up* with the Eldresses?"

"There must have been, some time, I suppose, but I suppose it was a very long time ago. And there's nothing at all in the Phrasebook anywhere about marriage services. It only talks about Brothers and Sisters looking after each-other, and Elders and Eldresses thinking on and directing the Hopeful efforts."

Jackson directed Mercy's hands farther downwards. "It sounds pretty ambiguous to me. So you don't want to get married then?"

"I've told thee, Jackson dearest, we're married already."

"Yes, but I mean – *officially*." Jackson himself wriggled now, recalling the looks he'd been getting in restaurants and stores and banks when he had Mercy around with him, and the number of calls from the wives of his fellow-Sherlockians, wanting to check through an audible layer of acid whether he'd be bringing his young house-guest to such and such a meeting or a dinner party. They hadn't merely seen, they had heard about Mercy.

After an initial, routine, swiftly aborted visit, the elastic encased thighs of Mrs Partington, his cleaning lady, had brushed each-other briskly out of his hallway and out of his life and into their station wagon.

Jackson had been made hideously aware of the vice that gripped Mrs Partington whenever she'd stooped to clean or polish, however cursorily, in his near vicinity over the past five years. She looked so frightening captured within her firm-control pantie girdle that he flinched to think what she'd be like if she were let out.

But Mrs Partington's mummified thighs got around, and so did her station wagon. *And* her scandalised opinion about the role in Jackson's house of Jackson's house-guest, lent weight to by the fact that not one of the spare beds had been slept in.

From the reactions he got lately, it seemed half the County was agog and the other half (the male half) was wondering how he did it.

Jackson discovered himself self-conscious, affected by public opinion, and surprisingly old-fashioned.

"Mercy," he choked, clutching her and dropping his scrap-pad, "*I* want to get married!"

Mercy folded her forehead up like a window blind. She said, "What difference would that make?"

This valid question, posed by men throughout the ages, was to Jackson as unanswerably threatening as a Black Hole. He applied to it all the logic used by those who'd wanted to get married before him.

"I don't know, I don't care!" He shook Mercy by her rounded upper arms till her apricot clothes and her lovely bosom wobbled. "I just want to, that's all!"

And Mercy, seeing in his desperate eyes his possible salvation, said, "I could only marry thee if Mother Germaine and the Eldresses were in agreement. They'd have to meet thee – I couldn't ever marry thee, dearest, unless thee became a proper, Pennsylvania Hopeful."

XXI

The big old house stood, pale and gracious, up on a hillside, with pink and gold rock plants tumbling away from it. Dogwood trees flanked it. Its ground rose to a clump of woods behind, and along one side – the north – the grass and buttercups were edged by beeches. To the south the hill dwindled, and at the front the curving slope of the driveway fell gently, gradually down to the road.

It was quiet and large, with room to work without being disturbed by vagrant noise from the kitchen. It was peaceful. It was isolated. It did not attract stray callers. It was a perfect house for a writer, provided the writer had someone to have sex with living in.

Jackson had someone to have sex with; he was sexually involved to the point of inextricability. To him Mercy was more than Hopeful – she was the resurrection and the life. And now, pottering amongst his memorabilia and ephemera, leafing through the latest Sherlock Holmes publications that were sent to him for reference or criticism, reading *The Baker Street Journal*, he was invested with a desire as throbbing and romantic as a preteenager's. Jackson saw himself at a white wedding. As a bridegroom: Jackson wanted to get married.

He saw himself eating home-made apple pies and casting sly glances at the bulge beneath Mercy's apron: he wanted to be a Daddy.

Out marketing, out visiting, other people's toddlers drew him like magnets. He peered into cots and car back seats and held forth a finger for tiny, sticky hands to grasp and said, "Ooochy-coochy-coo."

He went to his doctor and was told not only that vasectomies were rarely reversible, but that he was fifty-seven and overweight and his sperm count *before* the operation might not have been all that inspiring.

If it hadn't been for the rose and gold bundle waiting back there in the house on the hillside, Jackson felt sure, driving home alone from his doctor's office, that he would have been condemned to unrelieved flaccidity out of sheer mortification. That he was not condemned to such a condition was all Mercy's adorable doing. Mercy. . . . He'd wanted Mercy to have his baby.

They could adopt, perhaps, but that wasn't the same thing. For him, fatherhood had become a definitely sexual urge. He wanted to know that he had got her pregnant – that at some time in *his* wide bed in *his* bedroom in *his* old house, *he* had put a baby inside *her*.

If ever a man wanted to put a brand on something that read, "This is mine", Jackson wanted to put that brand on Mercy. And a womb full of a baby of his seemed to him the best brand he could think of. He was, he realised more clearly every day, truly terrified of losing her.

That she might somehow slip away from him, that her glowing love for him might be snuffed out, that this new existence in which he had more sex in a day than he'd had in months of his life with Sylvia – that this new existence might *end* – the nightmare edged out of his subconscious in the night when he was up, in more ways than one, making hot drinks and sandwiches. Mercy must be fettered, ensnared, trapped, bolted away and tied down. Mercy, if she couldn't be made pregnant, must at least be married. She must be known to be and seen to be legally his.

Jackson, who hitherto had been fairly liberal, became a real hard-core jealous male-chauvinist pig. He noticed that other men stared at Mercy, and mentally stripped her, and he took violent exception to their peeling looks. He glowered at other drivers if they eyed Mercy at stop lights. He interposed himself between Mercy and male passers-by. One weekend, when his agent had made the trip out from the city, to relax and bother Jackson about his manuscript, Jackson found himself leaving all his doors open. His agent had brought with him no female companion (this could only be due to an oversight or a social disease) and Jackson distrusted his agent in matters of women. If he had to leave Mercy alone with that fornicator, at no matter what distance, even far ends of the property, he was keeping his eyes and ears and the doors wide open. His agent returned to New York with an immovable shoulder, which he bitterly accused Jackson of causing by summer-night draughts.

Jackson delighted in Mercy so much that he imagined every other man in the State must share his enthusiasm and be rabid to leap on her. Waiters, cab drivers, delivery men – they were all suspect. Pharmacists, slavering behind high drug-store counters, couldn't wait to rip open their white coats and shove Mercy down on the ground and have her. Jackson carried this last belief to such conclusions that he insisted upon standing protectively right beside Mercy when she approached male drug-store assistants, to buy certain necessary items at certain times of the month.

Jackson even distrusted women: they could infect Mercy with modish ideas of morality; they might even be predatory, and Lesbian.

No amount of logical self-rebuke could alter his feelings. Jackson attempted to rationalise, and discuss things calmly with his ego: his symptoms were those of fear, and dread, and terror. So? There was only one way to ease this tormenting uncertainty – short of getting her pregnant which would of course have been the ideal. He couldn't lock her up completely (although that had, not unnaturally, occurred to him – Mercy being tethered like a pretty little white goat in the garden, to ramble amongst the shrubbery until he brought her in, in the evening); Mercy simply *must* be married.

To all this, which might by any less docile creature have been taken as harrassment, Mercy lent a cosy bosom, a sympathetic ear and a Hopeful countenance. She was willing to be married. If Jackson thought it was important, then she thought it was important. Whatever was important to dearest Jackson was important to her. She loved Jackson. Much more than that, she adored him.

And she wanted to save his soul, too, and she wanted to be married to a saved, secure Hopeful. Preferably in the open sight of the whole Sisterhood.

"*How*?" ranted Jackson. "You told me yourself, the Society doesn't have the facilities! It's impossible! You don't have any priests there, you don't have any ministers, you don't have any judges – you don't have marriages! Couldn't we just go ahead and send them a piece of cake and the photographs?"

But, always, at this juncture Mercy would burst into tears or serve him with a slice of Shoo Fly Pie. Sometimes she did both, simultaneously. If only he would come down to the settlement, Mother Germaine could advise them. She and the dear, wise Eldresses would be sure to know what was right to do.

* * *

It was not, Jackson acknowledged (in the intervals, tearing his grey hair over his manuscript), it was not that he objected to becoming Hopeful. So long as he could be Hopeful where he was, in his comfortable house on a hillside in New York State. It was the idea of the settlement and all it implied that nauseated him. Full of starched and sex-starved old maids and no electric light and no telephones – and no hot running water. (Mercy had made the grave mistake of letting that out one connubial, happy day in the bathroom.) And no mirrors. Mercy might disapprove of them, but Jackson was driven into paroxysms of ecstasy watching her reflection. He was (x-ing out a paragraph) driven into paroxysms of ecstasy by just about everything she did.

He would convert and become Hopeful if that meant he could get her snugly married, but the settlement and the starched Society were out – right out.

Even now he had to take his 'phone off the hook after lunch because of all the threatening calls from his agent. And the threatening calls weren't about his agent's shoulder. Where was the manuscript? *Where* was the manuscript? *Where the Hell was the manuscript*?

To interrupt the flow, to disrupt the creative process, to emerge from the book and go off down to Pennsylvania at this point, when all the threads in the narrative were coming together –

"Would thee like some coffee, dearest?" Mercy had come up behind him in a rustle of sweet-scented cotton. She put sachets of lavender and dried flowers in amongst all her clothes.

Her wide eyes gazed at him; she waited patiently for his answer. The sun streaming through the windows outlined her body and legs within the light print.

Jackson had never known so many vital interruptions to occur in his creative flow.

XXII

One early evening, when Jackson was out seeing a man about a new car in Millerton, Mercy sat in a sunchair in the garden and looked out over the view. She had mended all there was to mend. She had dusted all there was to dust – even the strange things that had to do with dearest Jackson's Sherlock Holmes man: the bottles of Baker Street Scotch Whisky and wine from Reichenbach; the busts of that funny looking person in that peculiar hat of his; the pipes that looked just like poor old dear Brother Orville's; the round glass you peeped through, that made everything seem bigger; the tobacco jar with 'Sherlock Holmes Tobacco' written on it; the packs of cards with pictures of dogs and odd names on; the buttons printed with 'Sherlock Holmes is alive and well at the Central Library'; all the bound volumes of *The Baker Street Journal*; all the faded, cracked old books; everything. Lamb was roasting in the oven, and the vegetables were prepared, and there was a pie cooling, and a deep bowl of cream whipped and waiting. . . .

The sky was molten pink, the green hills becoming blue with the approach of nightfall. The house looked across to a range Jackson had told her were called, he thought, the Shawangunks. Heathen names. . . .

She heard from all around the surge of pure bird song; the birds were calling goodnight to one another. Soon the owls would begin to hoot. The evening was so still here, and it was beautifully fresh out in the garden while the tall old house held the stuffy heat of the day.

What could she do? What? Jackson wanted to marry her, well that was all right in itself. Scour the Phrasebook as she might, she could find nothing actually against it. But simply marrying him wouldn't save him from Hellfire, and without the Society how could she convert him? She couldn't convert him all by herself. He seemed to be ripe for conversion, he read all the Phrases – he'd even copied out some of them – but *if only* he'd agree to visiting the settlement. Surely the Godliness of it would strike him as soon as he set foot inside the fencing?

Mercy moaned, and dabbed at a tear with her oven mitt. Mother Germaine would know what to do, *if only* she could go and see her. She had written to Mother Germaine, and Jackson had mailed the letter for her, and Mother Germaine had replied in her perfect script, "God bless thee, dear child. Bring home thy convert."

There was no getting round it: she wanted to go back, Mother Germaine wanted her to go back, but she couldn't go back without Jackson.

Mercy got up and began idling about the garden, slapping at her thigh with the oven mitt and then stooping guiltily to pluck out weeds. It was a sin to be idle. The Phrasebook said *Do not take they Recreation Hours lying down*.

She frowned over that for a minute. Could what she and Jackson did be called Recreation? But then the Phrasebook said one should spend one's Recreation Hours energetically, so that made it all right, if it was Recreation.

If Jackson didn't want to go to the settlement, how could she make him? She went and sat on the sunchair again, although the sun had left it and it was in shadow. The only *power* she had over Jackson (and she cringed from the Worldly word) was the fact that he loved her. He wanted to marry her, he never wanted her to go away. He kept saying that, over and over.

Supposing he thought she might go away, that she might leave if he wouldn't at least visit the settlement. . . .

But she absolutely hated arguments and quarrels, she didn't like upsetting him, if she started saying she'd go she knew he'd only persuade her not to, or he might stop her some way – that was no good. The only thing would be to really go. To go without telling him beforehand. To go somewhere he'd never ever think she'd dare go. To show him that she could do it. So that he'd know she might do it again, if he didn't do what she wanted. The faintest of breezes trembled through the beech leaves.

Mercy started breathing again. She felt herself start breathing.

She had actually stopped breathing. She had been so afraid she had stopped breathing. The thought, the notion of going somewhere alone. . . .

Out from here – how did you get out and away from here? She had only been out with Jackson, driven in his car. Except for one morning, the one morning she had gone for a walk, not long after he'd first brought her here to Pleasant Valley. The house was clean and he'd been working. And the day had been hot and still and fine. She had walked down the hillside and across the roadway, and taken a turning that wound between banks heavy with ferns and vine and daisies. After a time the turning had widened, and led past gates, and then past houses, and there had been dogs that had run and jumped and barked and howled at her, and one dog – a big black dog – that hadn't been chained up had rushed out of his front yard and crouched there snarling behind her, so she couldn't go back, and she had run and run and run. And then a car had stopped and a lady had picked her up and driven her back to Jackson's house, and told her it wasn't safe to walk down that road because all the house-owners kept fierce dogs, what with their places being so isolated; was she staying at the Jackson house, well, my goodness.

That day Jackson had given her a glass of *brandy*, and since then she'd never gone out alone, not without him, not any farther than the end of the driveway.

How could she go?

Jackson, one morning when his car made a funny noise, had telephoned for a taxi cab.

Mercy stood up and walked into the house. Her hands were clenched tight on the oven mitt.

There in the hall was the oval polished table, and there beside the 'phone was the message pad, and the pencil, and the booklet with all the special numbers in it. You just opened the cover and there were – she opened the cover – the numbers. Against 'Doctor' and 'Taxi cab' and 'Fire'.

And Jackson kept a train time-table, she knew he kept a train time-table. He had looked in it for that man, his agent, because his agent had said how long did it take to come out by train from New York City, and then he'd said not the Harlem line, my God. But it wasn't the Harlem line, Jackson had said that. He'd said the Hudson line, that was the easiest, to Poughkeepsie and then back from Poughkeepsie.

She walked out of the hall and into the large, light room Jackson used as a study. The setting sun had turned its walls golden orange. All the things she had dusted earlier were gold.

In the rack on his desk were all sorts of pamphlets – envelopes, newspaper clippings – and a little green-printed paper that read 'Poughkeepsie, Beacon, Cold Spring and Garrison – Grand Central Terminal, New York'.

New York. Her blood froze. It lay in her veins, not moving, solid. But if this was the only way to save Jackson's soul – *Hope is a lantern, get it out and raise it up*. Grudgingly, her blood began flowing.

She would go to New York. She would get a train there for Philadelphia, and in Philadelphia she would get a train for Lancaster.

"Ooooo –" Dribbles ran out of her mouth. She quavered with terror. But it must be done. She must run away. She would run away tomorrow. As soon as that. Before she lost her nerve.

Could she get as far as Lancaster? Could she get as far as Philadelphia?

There was the money left over from her Society Hill wages, that ought to be enough – that ought to be plenty. But in New York, the thought of changing trains!

No field is too large for the Hopeful plough.

Suppose she got as far as New York, couldn't she ask people. . . .

"Oooooo –" Her fingers were dead white on the paper and the oven mitt. She couldn't, no, no, she couldn't!

But there was Jackson's soul to save, and there was the Society to save, and there was Mother Germaine, and there were all the Eldresses. And, oh, just to be back home in the safe settlement.

Mercy sank down in one of dearest Jackson's soft, wide chairs. The little green-lettered paper had got crumpled but now she smoothed it out. The trains seemed to start running quite early – why, there was a train before six in the morning. She could see what the columns meant, it was all plain, thank goodness, under broad headings reading 'Leave' and 'Arrive'.

G.C.T.? That must mean – she turned the paper over, her hands were shaking – Grand Central Terminal. And Monday to Friday, except holidays. Whose holidays? Well, this wasn't holidays, and tomorrow was a Wednesday.

If she telephoned for a cab. . . . She'd heard Jackson do that, he called it booking a cab, and that meant you told them where you were and when they should come. Mrs Hiscock Mincham Muschamp used to do it in Society Hill too. Whenever she'd forgotten where she'd left her Mercedes.

If she telephoned now, before Jackson got in, she could ask for the cab to come early tomorrow morning – but then he'd hear it, he'd hear it coming for her! No, no. Mercy twitched, and nibbled the oven mitt stitching. *How*?

She'd ask the cab to come to the end of the driveway. And she wanted to catch – her quivering fingers ran down the columns – the eight-oh-seven train. That'd mean leaving – when? Very long before Jackson was stirring?

She'd ask the cab people. She'd say, "I have to catch the eight-oh-seven train from Poughkeepsie".

Mercy's teeth chattered. She'd have to pack. What? She'd have to pack something, even if it was only a change of underwear. And the Phrasebook – she mustn't forget the Phrasebook.

And in the morning she'd have to creep out of bed without disturbing Jackson – but he was used to her creeping out of bed to fetch him his breakfast. In his sleep, his plump hand rested over her waist and he curled her into his lap in an L-shape. And sometimes he snored a little. But not very much. When she crept out of bed to get him his breakfast, his hand always held on to her a little and then slithered away, and he rolled over like a cuddly toy and took the bed clothes with him. And when she came up with the tray he would make funny wuggle-wuggle noises and rub his eyes on the sheet and squint up at her, and then beam as though he'd been given a birthday present. And he would stretch up in the bed to kiss her good morning, and then she would slip into the big bed beside him, so they could eat the toast or the eggs or the muffins, and drink the tea or the coffee, together.

Oh, how could she possibly do this terrible thing? And how it would hurt him! Dearest, dearest Jackson, who had only ever been so good to her! She rocked backwards and forwards, chewing the train time-table and the oven mitt.

Hopeful Sisters, watch and tend to thy menfolk. Thy menfolk are open to the wiles of the Devil, and the World's snares. Most especially if they follow the Society's teaching, and wear trousers with a barn-door fastening.

It was all for the good of his soul. It was to save Jackson's soul, and it would hurt her as much as it would hurt him, but she had to do it.

Whimpering to herself and dribbling, Mercy went back out to the hall, opened the 'phone numbers booklet, lifted the receiver and stuck a wet forefinger in the telephone dial. The telephone made strange, frightening noises.

It was – it had to be – for the good of his soul.

XXIII

There was something different. As soon as Jackson woke up, he knew it. He felt it. Something different and something wrong. The bed felt different. The room smelled different. The house was different. He lay there and called out "Mercy?"

It was lighter – much lighter than usual. He'd slept later. Mercy hadn't woken him. There were no smells of breakfast, or coffee.

He sat up and called out "Mercy?"

He was naked, and became conscious of his nakedness in a way that he hadn't been since the first time he'd had her: conscious of his own flesh, that it was pale and there was too much of it. A fifty-seven year old man alone in a house. He was alone in the house. He knew it.

"Mercy?"

He got up, jerkily. His movements were stiff, he felt exposed – as though the room could laugh at him. The mirrors reflected him. A short man with a round stomach. How could he have wanted mirrors.

He found a robe in the bathroom and padded down the stairs in his bare feet. He could hear his puffing breath, little squeaks of anxiety, her name over and over.

The rooms hurried him on from one to another, as though he were unwelcome in all of them. What was he doing there, alone? Unhandsome, grey haired man who'd thought he'd found his youth again – the youth he'd never had, never enjoyed, never imagined till a door had been opened to him in Society Hill, Philadelphia, by a little blonde who blushed and wore no make-up.

He ran out into the garden, and cut his foot on a pebble.

"Mercy! Mercy!" The name floating out over the trees, across the roadway. He stood there in his robe, his stocky legs ridiculous beneath it, with his feet – one cut and stinging – down there in the grass of his lawn.

It had all been a dream. She had been a dream. She had never existed. He had wanted her so much he had conjured her up. He'd been running a fever ever since Philadelphia.

But when he limped back into the house, he found traces of her. There were traces of Mercy in every room; mementoes of her everywhere. Her mending, left in a neat stack. Fresh-scented linen in all the cupboards. The immaculate ironing. Her girlish clothes in the wardrobes. The plain soap she liked. The soup stock on the stove. And a note against the coffee pot. Which read: "Dearest Jackson, I love thee but I cannot go on living with someone who isn't Hopeful. I am going to New York and if God helps me I will get to Lancaster. My faith is in the settlement. Thine sincerely, Mercy."

New York! So his damned blasted agent had got at her – his damned blasted fornicating fucking agent! He'd probably told her he'd look after her – Jackson tore to the telephone, and then remembered. His agent never got up before noon, and it was only ten twenty.

She could be there by now. Two hours before he poured the orange juice on his stomach lining. He'd never have arranged –

She'd gone off to New York *all by herself*?

Dear God, Mercy would become another morgue statistic!

* * *

By a miracle, Jackson caught the ten fifty-six from Poughkeepsie (the ticket clerk remembered the little Hopeful vividly), and as he fought his way off the train an hour later he fell over Mercy, who was sitting in the gloom and crying on a carpet bag.

She had been stranded in the stale air and the dank, subterranean, sallow lighting since ten eleven. There hadn't been any red caps, and every train-load of passengers had streamed right on past her, and she hadn't been able to find her way up from the tracks! She threw herself into his arms, and Jackson gave her a handkerchief. He was thankful he hadn't had to wait for the twelve fifty-six.

He took her away and bought her an ice-cream, and afterwards they travelled straight back on the two fifty. Jackson held her hand all the journey. When he could speak, he said, "I promise you, Mercy, but you mustn't ever, ever do anything like that again." He heard the sound of his own swallowing. "I promise you I'll become a Hopeful."

"Thee'll become a Hopeful in the settlement? Thee promises thee'll come back with me for a visit so I can introduce thee?"

"I promise you, I promise you anything. For God's sake don't ever leave me again."

They looked at each-other, the blonde with the huge eyes and the round man with the grey hair. His tie was crooked and her green dress was very rumpled. And Jackson said, "For God's sake, Mercy, don't look at me like that, darling. I'm fifty-seven and we're sitting here in public. For God's sake, don't make me cry."

Part Seven

She also lieth in wait as for a prey, and increaseth the transgressors among men.

XXIV

"Aw –" Twatchel was going through *The Hound of the Baskervilles* with an eraser. "Aw, what'd you put rings round this for, you know what an Eskimo is!"

"Of course I know what an Eskimo is. They sit in the snow with those beautiful furs on, and they fish in the ice with those things, those poles. Will thou do me up at the back?"

"Aw –"

"Don't thou be silly, Twatchel."

"Aw –"

"Twatchel Clootie, will thou come over here!"

"Aw –" Twatchel shambled over, and did her up at the back at arms' length, ineptly, handicapped because he was averting his eyes.

"I didn't put rings round Eskimo, there was some other word." She wriggled her shoulders. "Thank thee, Twatchel. I know it was some other word. Here, let me see –"

"No! D'you *realise* how much that edition cost me?" Twatchel, released from his duty at Grace's straining fastenings, loped to interpose his body between her and his precious *Hound of the Baskervilles*. "That's a rare book, and you've been touching it, making those rings again! Those rings are *unnecessary*!" He opened the afflicted volume, using the tips of his fingers, and closed it again, shuddering. "D'you *always* have to press so deep with your pencil? After I rub out the lines, I can still see the marks!"

Grace rolled her eyes and said, "Oh, *Twatchel*."

"Conan Doyle spelled Eskimo 'E-s-q-u-i-m-a-u-x'. You only have to say the word out loud to work out what it means."

"I couldn't say it out loud, I didn't know how to say it!"

"Aw –"

"And thou can stop being such an old grouch, thou'll stick that way if the wind changes." She looked down at herself and appeared satisfied. "I told thee where I've left thy supper."

Twatchel sniffed.

"There's nothing to heat through, so thou can't boil it over. Oh, and I meant to ask thee, what's the Blair House?"

"The Blair House?" Twatchel reared into his mobile crane imitation. "I pointed it out the first day you got here, when I was driving you from Union Station. It's the official guest house across from the White House. Where they accommodate visiting Heads of State, that kind of people. There's some Arab, someone like that – potentate, leader – he's there right now, and his entourage."

"Oh?" Grace glanced at him quickly. "What's entourage?"

"Staff. Servants, advisers."

She held up her arms so the slender gold bracelets cascaded down them. "Some Arab?"

"Some mid-East high-up, who knows? How should I know, all I have are the maps and the flags and the maximum tonnage!"

"Don't be so crabby, Twatchel. Thou'll get that nervous eczema again and have to cover thyself in cold cream."

"It wasn't –"

"The *mess* in thy pyjamas." She wrinkled her nose. "Well, I'm going out now."

"Good!"

She smiled at him, a red-headed bully with cleavage, his mother with nipples, and stuck out her tongue.

Funny old Twatchel. Funny how he wasn't old, but he behaved like it. Grace sauntered towards Pennsylvania Avenue. Her showered, powdered skin was already filming with sweat in the heat.

So that was what the Blair House was. B.W.'d said about it being important. And that wasn't all he'd said. Pulling things to pieces. . . .

She tossed her head crossly, unconsciously. He'd been drinking, he did that so much now, and he'd said it like an insult, not an invitation. "A party at the Blair House. Saturday, Grace. Just your style." And he'd kicked a table over: a long low glass table; the plants had been spoiled and the glasses had spilled. "We've been asked to find some girls who'll go to it. Do you understand me, Grace? Girls who'll go to it? Girls who don't mind a little fun, Grace. Girls who are really friendly."

She'd watched him. She hadn't moved to the spilled things. The amount he drank these days, and he was unpredictable – moody. He wasn't moody in bed, though. When he ever got there.

"You go along and you'll have a good time, I'll arrange it so they'll expect you." B.W.'s eyes were reddened, staring. "He's important, that man at the Blair House. We want to make him happy. We want to make them all happy, Saturday they're having a private party."

"Are thou coming?"

"No." He'd turned his back on her. His broad back. He'd put a shirt on, otherwise he was naked. "They've got enough men, it's more girls they need." He finished his drink – she heard the ice clinking – and then he said, "Don't worry, there'll be men without me. Plenty of men. Just how you like it. That's how you like it, isn't it, half dozen cocks at a time?"

Not that again. She should never have told him.

"And they'll know you know me, Grace, they'll know you're not prejudiced. Anything, just as long as the numbers are right? The numbers'll be right for you, Grace. You might get lucky, you may even come twice."

She'd taken a cab home. Getting out had been the only way to handle him these past weeks. And the times he was worst were when she'd been with Mr Saetiger. It was almost as though he *knew* about the Potomac Plaza. But he couldn't, of course he couldn't, how could he? John Roberts Jobsdock's guest of the Government – Semyon was secret. John had explained to her, and he had used the word discretion; she mustn't tell anyone she was seeing Mr Saetiger. That was no trouble, she was careful with B.W. anyway. But the Government guest and him – she kept their dates apart especially carefully.

If she couldn't avoid it, if she had to see both of them, it was

B.W. she saw first and then she made an excuse and left him. But B.W. was strange, awfully quiet when she did that.

Today he'd 'phoned, sober, and confirmed the thing at the Blair House. He'd sounded very far away, very depressed and unhappy. She tossed her head again. B.W. and his stupid hangovers.

* * *

Under a sun umbrella, the inexhaustible Israeli member was waiting. Menachem. She'd been meeting him more, since B.W. had become so difficult. All his features were large, his smile split his big-boned face wide open, and he kept his thick dark hair short, he'd once told her, because it continually stood up on end.

They had a few drinks, and he flirted with her – he always flirted with her, he seemed to think it was necessary – and to have something new to talk about she told him about the party at the Blair House.

"You're going *where*?" he shouted. People at other tables turned round and looked at them.

"I'm going to a party there, don't shout! What's the matter with thee?"

"What's the matter with *me*? What's the matter with *you*! You want your head examined? Do you know what they *do*?" He pushed his face towards her; all of the other tables were silent now, listening "They do it in *groups*! They do it in *tribes*! They do it *holding hands* together! And *the way* they do it! You think they sit around eating sheeps' eyeballs and messing up Jerusalem? Heh? You think that's all? You think that's all they do? That's *nothing*! A friend of mine travelled on a 'plane from Bahrein, there was a sheikh and his people in first class with the stereo equipment – they'd never even seen a lavatory! What's wrong with you?" He leant back again; he slapped his own forehead. "You don't want to live long, or something? What's a decent girl like you doing at a party like that?"

"I don't –"

"And who's entertaining them, heh? Who's asked you to this party?" His nose and mouth formed a sneer. "Someone working for the Government?"

"Well –"

"You know what that means! A party like that, it means what it always means! The FBI."

"Well, I suppose –"

"You suppose! And I suppose Josef Mengele was a good doctor! The FBI – pimps, procurers!" He hammered on the table, so that the drinks jumped about and slopped over. "Pimps for the Arabs, pimps for the Fascists, pimps for the Communists so they can get the pictures! Them and the CIA – pimps and procurers!"

"Ummm," said Grace. "Menachem, can I have another white wine spritzer?"

* * *

It was early when they parted – earlier than either of them had expected. Menachem had been so affected he'd been incapable for the first (and, he was later reassured to find, the last) time. But as a consequence Grace arrived an hour before she'd thought she would at the Potomac Plaza, and learned that Mr Saetiger had been going out for a nice little drive. They would both go out, said Semyon, with the decision of Mount Rushmore. And his driver cruised them to Potomac Park, so they could have an evening stroll around.

The driver sat in the car while they admired the Jefferson Memorial. He sat directly between and beneath the two microphones, and considerably forward of the concealed floor container holding the recording machinery and the tape spools. The tapes ran whenever he had to drive Saetiger anywhere, although there was rarely anything of note on the spools when they were taken from the car.

Grace and Saetiger were walking and talking and turning their heads to one-another, so if anyone surveilling them had been filming it was unlikely their lips could have been read.

But no-one was filming. No-one was watching them, except the driver and one other person, who'd got out of his car to amble about just as they were.

And they weren't expected to be saying anything very important. They said nothing very important inside the Potomac Plaza; the tapes that were made of all they said testified to that. Semyon Saetiger was a laconic man, who regarded women as a sexual necessity, and sometimes pretty, not potential conversationalists, and Grace was a willing, complaisant companion for him. The girl did not take drugs and was only a moderate drinker. She was promiscuous, that had been established. It was also necessary. She would occasionally arrive more ready to respond to Saetiger, after seeing some other casual lover. They never discussed this; they had no discussions. Certainly there was nothing to warrant such detailed surveillance as a camera team and lip reading.

And so it was that no-one at any position in the net between Semyon Saetiger and John Roberts Jobsdock, or anyone for rings and rings around *him*, came to know that Grace politely warned the guest of the Government she wouldn't be able to see him the following Saturday evening, because she was going to a party. Nor that Saetiger expressed gloom, because Saturday was his birthday. Nor that Grace thought a little while and then said the party was for guests of the Government and he was a guest of the Government, and she was sure that'd make it O.K., and why not come along.

And thus the topic, unobserved, was quickly settled and dealt with.

Saetiger had been contemplating her breasts and her stomach as he stalked beside her, and made Grace walk in front of him now, a way, so he could watch her behind moving. And next said he wanted to go back to the apartment, no more walking. They sat in the car together; the driver was aware Saetiger had his hands inside the girl's panties on the back seat, and when they arrived at the Potomac Plaza the driver was immediately dismissed. The tapes for that hour in the apartment recorded very little but noises.

* * *

Around about the time Grace was parading in front of Mr Saetiger, and thinking how elegant the Jefferson Memorial really was, her friend Menachem was having a drink with someone he knew from Channel Seven. And demanding deflatedly whether *something* shouldn't be done about it, when Arabs were being provided by the FBI with girls!

And being told that what people did for fun was their own business. Provided what they did was behind their own doors.

"Are you telling me the Israeli legation live like a bunch of celibates?" Carl wiped his wrists. "You're just jealous, that's all, because that redhead of yours with the knockers –"

"That's not the issue! Who says she's my redhead!"

"Well, so what's your worry, let them get on with it."

XXV

John Roberts Jobsdock was dining at the Rive Gauche when he got the message. It was not entirely unusual for him to be interrupted at dinner, but interruptions of that sort seldom heralded good.

"Yes?" he said coldly, having determined it was a menial.

"She's taken him in the Blair House."

John Roberts Jobsdock hung like an icicle. Several lifetimes later he spoke into the receiver and said "Burick, this is not a secure line."

"Security, shiturity. I'm telling ya she's taken him in the Blair House. There some kinda party going on there?"

Johsdock reeled numbly through his cerebral card index. "There's a mid-East Head of State, whole entourage, some kind of –" His fingers were translucent stalacmites on the 'phone. "Wing-ding . . . Jesus Christ. Jesus *Christ*!"

"Yeah."

"How did it happen? How did you let it happen, you *idiot*?"

"There's no need to call people names."

"You're supposed to be taking care of him, what are you *doing*?"

"I wasn't doing nothing! I was following him in the second car, like always, I was using the Rabbit. I'm parked outside the apartment, she gets out a cab about eight thirty, well usually that means –"

"I know what it means!"

"So I'm surprised, she comes down with him, it'd be twenty minutes later, they're breaking records, and there's a cab there. Another cab. They musta called one. Didn't use Milt, didn't call him, I checked."

"Jesus *Christ*."

"Yeah. So I thought, maybe they're going somewhere, having some kinda intimate dinner, maybe it's some place, you know, it's a bit naughty, somewhere he'd be embarrassed to have his driver take him –"

"Get on with it, Burick!"

"So I'm surprised, the cab stops outside the Blair House. Out she gets, out he gets, he pays off the cab, and they're in."

"Do you mean to tell me they weren't *prevented*?"

"It looked to me, the way it went, she was expected. She was flapping her hands around him a coupla seconds, that's all I saw."

"They walked in? They just *walked in*? You –" John Jobsdock's brain suddenly turned up a name on the card index. He read it, in letters of frost, in silent agony. Benjamin Williams. Benjamin Williams! *Benjamin Williams*! He would have howled it aloud, but his throat was choked up with snowflakes.

Burick said, "Yeah. I park and I wait, nothing happens, no-one comes out again. Lotsa girls going in though."

"You *waited*?" John Jobsdock whimpered. "Burick, *how long ago* did this happen?"

"Maybe – I'd say an hour. Maybe longer."

"An *hour*!"

"Yeah. Well, like I said, I waited ta see did they come out. And then I hadda find you."

"You found me!" John Roberts Jobsdock held himself together; his teeth were chattering. "Answer me one question, Burick. *What are you doing in Washington*?"

"I'm tailing the –"

"I don't mean that! I mean, why did they send you here from wherever it was you came from?"

"Oh, yeah. I had my depression."

"*What*?"

"Depression. All the time, I had to take these tablets. Terrible. I got claustrophobia. It was the way I was living – casinos, casinos. And my wife didn't like it, it was unhealthy hours."

"Burick!"

"Yeah."

"Get back *immediately*!" The cerebral card index had frozen on Benjamin Williams. "I – I'm – I'm coming right over there."

But unfortunately, Burick couldn't get back immediately. He found the Rabbit boxed in by another parked car, and the parked car was a White House Cadillac.

And John Roberts Jobsdock couldn't go right on over there, because the lady he was dining with didn't like his explanation for leaving her, and the lady he was dining with was a Southern Senator's wife.

The people who got there immediately were a tired and grimy Channel Seven news team, on their way in from covering a fire. They were tuned to the sporadic bursts of the police wavelength and heard the squawked report of a disturbance outside the Blair House.

One of the tired news team opened his sore eyes a millimetre, and leaned forward to tap the driver on the shoulder. "Get over there," he said.

"*What* the Hell –"

"I'm telling you. Get over there." Carl lay back again, and briefly closed his eyes. Something and nothing. . . .

Of the two options, it turned out to be something. The station wagon crammed with the roving TV news team arrived the same time as the prowl cars. Nobody missed being affected. Everybody's eyes opened. Everybody's ears opened. Everybody's mouth opened. Some brains fell out.

The balmy night was rent with a deafening noise and a dazzling vision. For some minutes, the thunderstruck watchers were rooted, pole-axed, in their cars. . . .

The sky was clear and the moonlight was bright, and if it hadn't been, there were the street lights and headlights. The roadway outside the Blair House was as spectacularly lit as the Hollywood Bowl.

And running and milling and shrieking around inside this flare path was a crowd of exceedingly nubile and furiously angry young women. It was possible to tell they were angry, the way they were screaming obscenities and throwing spare manacles at the windows of the Blair House.

"My *God*," whispered the Channel Seven driver. "My *God*!"

The girls were an undulating sea of scoops of multi-flavoured ice-cream, pink and white and cream and fudge and chocolate, every wave bouncing and jouncing and jostling and rippling. Blonde and brunette and platignum and strawberry and sherry – and very few of them natural. And all of them, every single one of them, every delicious flavour, as naked as the day they were born.

"Oh Holy Mother," moaned a patrolman. "Oh Holy Mother, why didn't I become a priest!"

With their bare skins, it was true, some of the girls wore quaint and fetching accessories. One of them was wrapped in a python.

One of them was weighted at the wrist by a trapeeze padded in velvet.

One of them was shouting at a German Shepherd, "Not now, you bastard, get down!"

There were a few with some remnants of clothes on – plastic, waterproofs, boots here and there, black leather.

One of them was wheeling a baby carriage, which was overflowing with musical instruments and bottles of Jergens lotion. Apparently unperturbed by the mêlée, this vision climbed on top of her baby carriage and, in the midst of the fracas, curled up amiably and fell fast asleep.

And one girl, a completely nude and truly notably stacked creamy skinned redhead, was attempting ineffectually to assist a square, bristly haired man. The man was not as naked or temptingly displayed as the young women; he had a cigar in his mouth and his undershorts on.

And Carl began to move for the first time when he saw him.

"It can't be!" he breathed. "It can't be. Menachem, I love you. I love you, Menachem, you hear me. It can't be. And it is!" And he leapt out of the station wagon, part of the amoebic structure of men and mikes and shouldered camera, and evaded a juiced up German Shepherd, and caught up with the redhead and said "Hi, Grace, you know me. You remember me – Carl? You came to a party with Menachem, over at my place, couple of weeks ago."

"Oh, yes," said Grace. "How are thou?" She seemed distracted. "Isn't it dreadful? I can't see thy watch, Semyon." The solid man with her was scouring the roadway, muttering, "Was good watch" and puffing out smoke round his butt of cigar.

"Isn't it dreadful, Carl? They threw us out in the street like this, just because we weren't *shaven*." She touched herself approvingly. "*Shaven*. Well. They started screaming and shouting and throwing handfuls of rice at the walls and they don't appreciate American hospitality *at all*. Not at all." She touched herself again. "Well, has thou ever heard anything like that in the whole of thy life? *Ever*?"

Carl shook his head solemnly. He knew the rest of the team were lining up the shot, and he was holding the microphone. He was fizzing with excitement, and an overwhelming desire to laugh. He was aware of Grace's bosom (he was closer to it than she was), and to his left a really staggering black girl, who was wearing only a narrow gold chain and kicking a policeman pretty hard in the crotch. The sound her heel made, connecting, was the sound of a baseball bat hitting a peach.

The sound the policeman made appeared on seismographs.

The scene in the brightly lit roadway outside the Blair House was something out of Hieronymus Bosch, but Grace, though stark naked, had now abandoned the watch search and remembered her manners. She put a hand under the solid man's elbow, and said "Carl, thou doesn't know Mr Saetiger."

"Oh yes I do!" said the grinning news man. "And *this* is Channel Seven." He straightened his face for the camera. "Hello, Mr Saetiger. Hello, again. And how are you, sir? Settling down in Washington? How are you finding it here, sir? " The zoom found Grace's breasts, within inches of the cigar butt. "What would it be now – December, January? We met about eight months ago, sir, didn't we? You remember – at the press conference, when you *defected*? "

Part Eight

How doth the city sit solitary, that was full of people! How is she become as a widow! She that was great among the nations, and princess among the provinces. . . .

XXVI

Jackson was packing when he got the call from Twatchel. For a time, all he could hear was screaming.

"Do you know what she's been *doing*?" Twatchel sounded like Cleo Laine sitting on a needle. "Do you *know* what she's been *doing*?"

Jackson cleared a space on the bed and made himself comfortable. He said, "You're obviously going to tell me."

"Don't you be cute with me, Jackson! You sent that infiltrator down here!"

"Infiltrator! That's a new name for it. Look, I knew the girl got around a little –"

"*Got around*! I have had the CIA here! And the FBI. And every time I move there are news men in the front yard. They're out there now, sitting playing poker in the grass! Jackson, the situation's impossible. I'm suspended – they've taken her away and they're keeping her in some hotel room – it doesn't look as though they can hold her for anything but they don't want her to talk to anybody. Aw – there's nobody left she hasn't talked to! And I'm not supposed to talk to anybody, they told me, but I'm talking to you! You're the first call I've made since I called my lawyer. Jackson, you have got to tell them I never knew her – you have got to tell them it was you sent her down here!"

"I already told them."

"*When*?"

"I told them in the middle of the night, last night. And they called here this morning, to see me in person. They took statements from Mercy too, they seemed satisfied. They're probably checking out the YWCA now. And that hotel in Philadelphia. For all I know they're checking out the settlement."

"Jackson, you've got to help me, they've taken away all my maps and my file system!"

"Have they taken your Holmes collection?"

"No, they're going through it here in the apartment. I've been warned, if they find anything subversive –"

"Well, there goes *The Valley of Fear*."

"Aw, it's all very funny for you up there, you've never taken Washington seriously!"

"Twatchel, *nobody* takes Washington seriously. Unless they live in Washington. You've got too many citizens inside there taking themselves seriously. Washington's its own ingrowing toenail. Washington must have the only population who could go into group therapy all by themselves. If the rest of us joined in we'd all be in the Violent Ward."

"Judas!"

Jackson held the receiver away from his head and said, "Come down an octave. Now, stop screaming and think a little. You're suspended, you said. What does that mean exactly?"

"It means what it says, I can't do anything."

"I suppose if you go anywhere you have to report to them?"

"Aw –"

"When they've finished checking you out and finding all you do is sit around the Pentagon planning to blow the world to smithereens, why don't you pack your bags and take a vacation?"

"Aw, well, I don't want to go and see my mother –"

"I'm not talking about your mother, Twatchel, I'm talking about the settlement."

"The *settlement*? What – that place in Pennsylvania where Grace came from You're not just irresponsible, Jackson, you're *crazy*! You probably organised this whole thing from the beginning, you want to overthrow society as we know it, you want the downfall of America!"

"Stop screaming, Twatchel! I have got to go to the settlement and I want some man around to talk to. Even you would do, Twatchel."

"Aw, thanks!"

"At least we read the same books."

There was a lot of static, and the sound of tapes churning. Then Twatchel said, "Do you think they'd let me?"

"I should think they'd be glad to get rid of you. From my understanding of the situation, practically anyone connected with Grace would do Washington a favour by going somewhere and lying low right now."

XXVII

Which was exactly right, as Twatchel Clootie discovered. Of course, not everyone was prepared to perform the favour, but there were those who had no option.

John Roberts Jobsdock, uninvited to take a seat, stood beside a desk and waited while a man with his back turned, a man who did not cease to gaze through the window, put Jackson's sentiments into more convoluted sentences.

There had also been general talk of overseas postings, to places as congenial as Helsinki and Guyana.

"A rest?"

"A rest," confirmed the man at the window. "A rest, John, somewhere very quiet."

Semyon Saetiger sat or stood or lay down stiffly in the new apartment – in the safe house to which they had moved him. The tapes recorded that he muttered. There was the occasional growl or shout. A translation confirmed that he was deeply offended, at his age, and in his position, to have had the woman taken away and replaced with worn out centre folds.

Benjamin Williams made it difficult for everybody; he didn't want to talk about anything, he simply resigned. His resignation was torn up in front of him and a vacation suggested. When he got home, he opened a new bottle, put on tapes of a Mozart piano concerto, and packed.

Various men in Government and The Red Circle picked up their things from where their wives had dumped them, in the street and in document shredders, and went and emptied bank accounts and deposit boxes and decided what they needed most in life was a place with no 'phone.

Grace was allowed out of purdah and back to Foggy Bottom. But no, she wouldn't go away anywhere. She was being contacted by something called media, and a very nice gentleman had asked her was she good at dancing.

The member of the Israeli legation was told Grace was home by the man from Channel Seven. Posing as the humble deliverer of a chopped liver and cottage cheese sandwich, he got past the journalists playing poker in the long grass and elicited the precise location of the settlement. He and Carl had decided to visit it. Partly business:

"*And from this quiet corner of Pennsylvania came the girl whose dramatic appearance on this Channel rocked all Washington, whose diplomatic connections have yet to be fully revealed, and whose forthcoming book will surely rock the world. The girl whose sizzling cabaret act is currently in preparation. . . .*"

And partly pleasure: "I'd really like to see the place, Carl, could be some kind of kibbutz, heh? Where they raised Grace, a schickse and she made fools out of the FBI and the Arabs! Is it possible, that Mother of hers ever met Golda Meir?"

Anne and Rose Mary thought it would be great to drive up to the settlement for a week with Carl and Menachem, and just think of the pictures.

There were repercussions even in Philadelphia. Mrs Cordelia Hiscock Mincham Muschamp was elected Chairperson of no less than fifteen committees, and Kegan Hiscock Mincham Muschamp took a partner into the practice so he could give interviews to *Esquire* in consulting hours.

The YWCA made it a policy decision to give no interviews.

Beatrice lost twenty pounds and went and married a journalist.

The hotel sacked the Personnel Manager.

XXVIII

The first interesting sight they saw, when Jackson turned into the dirt road beside the spotless fencing of the settlement, was a black man in a silk shirt and gaberdine dungarees, with a radio hung round his neck, painting an outhouse.

The next interesting sight was a group of men – mixed colours, some tall, some short, some in jeans, some in Bermuda shorts, some in great distress – chasing a cow. And the cow was winning.

The third sight they saw was an urbane uncomfortable looking pale man in a well cut suit that was getting very dirty, up on the roof fixing the shingles.

The fourth sight they saw was a tall figure with sandy hair and wild elbows, pegging out a line of long blue linen washing.

"My *God*," said Jackson, his forehead on the windshield. "That is *Twatchel*!"

"Ooo, dearest," wailed Mercy. "Ooo, dearest, it's so different!"

Dearest took his head off the windshield, his foot off the brake and didn't say anything at all.

When they pulled up, no-one came out of the Society House to meet them. There was hardly room to park the car.

Mercy clambered out, and Jackson heaved himself after her (because of the number of vehicles, they both had to get out the same side). On the porch, Mercy spied Sister Agatha sitting in her rocker. She did not look as though she should be disturbed. She was typewriting very heatedly on a machine.

Up the steps, across the porch and into the hallway. . . . The scent of boiled greens, and wax, and lemon verbena. Sister Unity's voice came echoing from above, somewhere, "Titty, *at once*, put down that cigar!"

In the dear, plain, shining hallway corridor, Mother Germaine was standing talking to a swarthy young man who was drumming his fists against the thighs of his white cord trousers. "No," she was saying firmly, "I am very sorry indeed, Brother Menachem, but it would be completely out of the question. The two young ladies are staying in one of our Eldresses' Rooms, and thou art staying in one of the Elders' Rooms, and that is final."

The young man hit himself quite hard. He hissed, "You remind me of my sister-in-law!"

Mother Germaine said "Oh my. Thank thee, dear."

Then she saw Mercy and said, "Child!" rather absently. And "So thou art back, how lovely." And "The Sisters will be so pleased."

Brother Menachem stamped away.

Mercy said "H-Hello, Mother Germaine." She felt nervous; there was something wrong, something missing somehow, she could feel. She said "This is dearest Jackson, Mother Germaine. Thee knows, I wrote –"

"Ah, yes. Thy convert." Mother Germaine fetched a book out of her hanging pocket and consulted it, vaguely. "My goodness, where are we going to put them all. It's beginning to look as though the barns –"

"But I've *brought him back*. Mother Germaine?" Mother Germaine couldn't have comprehended –

"Yes, so I see, child." Mother Germaine inclined her head guardedly at Jackson. "Even one convert is welcome in the Hopeful Society of Faith in the Continual Resurrection."

"*Even* one convert!" By now Jackson was also ruffled. He shouldered up to her and said aggressively "How d'you know it's only going to be one convert? It may turn out to be quad converts! I'm still trying to have the operation reversed! It won't be Mercy's fault if nothing happens!"

Mother Germaine sighed and tapped at her book.

"I came all the way down here just to please her, she wanted your approval so we could be married! I think that's fantastic of her. So what's wrong with *one convert*!"

"Nothing. Except in comparison." Mother Germaine gestured towards the open door behind them, to the parked cars and the populated pastures of the overcrowded, seething settlement. "In comparison to the work in the World of that saintly evangelist –"

XXIX

The lights dimmed, all but the white spot with the pink filter. The compere stepped forward on the small stage, his teeth blinding, his cologne palpable amongst the clustered tables.

"And now I have to introduce to you," he purred. "Ladies and gentlemen. The sensational act, the top of the bill here –"

Concealed from the audience, Grace took a deep breath and tweaked at her G-string. She hummed softly to the music they were using. It'd be better when she'd had the whole Phrasebook orchestrated. Up to now there weren't enough Phrases ready, and the band had to fill in with that old tune. Still. . . . They seemed to pay more attention to her dancing than anything else. All that practise she'd had doing the dancing (for Unity! she giggled) in the boring, starchy Recreation Hour. . . .

"The one you've all been talking about! The one you've all been waiting for! The girl who makes Bette Midler look shy! That staggering, electrifying, sensationally sexy little lady –"

Grace licked her lips, and checked on her nipples.

"That one-girl Watergate – AMAZING GRACE!!"

Sayings from The Phrasebook of Uplift

No field is too large for the Hopeful plough.

All the World's a quilt, and Hopeful men and women merely quilters.

Turn thy back on the World and keep thy front for the Hopeful.

To be Hopeful is a state of mind. With God's help it may lead to a physical condition.

Put thy hand on that which is important to thee and it will profit thee in the World.

A Hopeful woman carries the yoke through life, and a Hopeful man carries the bridle.

The Hopeful shall inherit all that the meek leave over.

A Hopeful countenance is a cheerful countenance. Even at a death bed, Hopefuls recall Lazarus.

Hope is a lantern. Get it out and raise it up and it will keep thee happy in the darkness.

Bake Hopefully, mend Hopefully, make Hopefully, and count thy change.

The morning is a Hopeful time, given sufficient molasses.

Hopeful Sisters, carefully tend to thy menfolk's clothing. The Devil waits in a slack fastening.

The Devil can resist everything but the Hopeful. The Hopeful should resist everything, just in case.

If thou shakest hands with the World, count thy fingers afterwards.

Spend thy Recreation Hours energetically. Simple pleasures should not be taken lying down.

If molasses be the food of Hope, bake on.

Never refuse money. It can always be washed.

To be Hopeful is a blessing. It is also necessary.

Acknowledgements

If it hadn't been for TWA, I wouldn't have got across the Atlantic, and if it hadn't been for the others listed here I might very well have spent the rest of my time in America trying to find my way out of Kennedy Airport. So, my warmest thanks and deep gratitude go to:–

TWA, for flying me smoothly, efficiently and very convivially to New York, and for trying to cram me with sufficient food en route to last me for at least a week after arrival. It was not their fault I developed acne through nerves at some high point above mid-Ocean.

Otto Penzler, for meeting me and preventing me from taking the next flight straight back. Despite having to be seen in public with someone who kept searching the stores for a yashmak, he devoted days of his energy and time to showing me round, answering my asinine questions, introducing me to delightful people – and only got us lost once, when I wanted to go for a ride on the Staten Island Ferry.

Judge and Mrs Albert M. Rosenblatt, who took me into their home in Pleasant Valley when I was too jet-lagged to say 'Hello' or 'Thank you', who were unfailingly kind, helpful and tolerant, and who not only provided me with a vast amount of vital research material but also let me stay in their bathroom as long as I wanted and let me sleep late every single morning. If there is a Purple Heart for hosts, they earned it.

Dr and Mrs Michael Kean, whose hospitality and guidance in Pennsylvania were the most wonderful surprise package I could possibly have received. Without the maps, information, chauffeuring services and common sense they lavished upon me, the book simply could not have been written.

Jon Lellenberg, who watched my being handed on down the Eastern Seaboard like a rather hot brick and who, despite all he must have heard, actually drove me to Washington, acted as my host there, and gave me the most intensive course on the city possible, considering the June temperatures.

To all these people, and to many others – Gail Patelcuis, Michelle Slung, Dee Knapp, Peter Blau, Dan Young – this book and I owe an enormous debt. Of course, another way of looking at it would be, having read the book, to hold all of them at least partly responsible. . . .